ELEVEN LITTLE ROBOTS

BOOK 4: The Robot Galaxy Series

Adeena Mignogna

ELEVEN LITTLE ROBOTS

Copyright © 2023 by Adeena Mignogna

This is a work of fiction. Names, characters, places, and incidents are the product of the author's imagination. Any resemblance to actual persons, living or dead, events, or locales, or actual robots, functioning or not, is entirely coincidental.

ISBN: 979-8-9855963-2-8 (paperback)

Edited by: Carolani Bartell

Book cover design by: Ebooklaunch.com

Published by Crazy Robot, LLC

The Robot Galaxy Series

Book 1: Crazy Foolish Robots

Book 2: Robots, Robots Everywhere!

Book 3: Silly Insane Humans

Book 4: Eleven Little Robots

DEDICATION

To all the people who helped me get this far.

Before We Begin

It is inevitable that once a species invents the wheel on their planet of origin, their evolution carries them through animal-drawn carriages, automobiles, and Segways, and onto rocket ships, treadmills, and cordless vacuum cleaners. It is during this evolutionary process that they start looking up at what else is happening around their host star. At first, their observations are confined to whatever visual sensors naturally evolved and are already embedded in their bodies, but as they advance, they utilize technology to resolve smaller and smaller details and answer bigger and bigger questions.

Barring complete self-destruction, it is inevitable that they find other planets around their star. Once again, initially with their natural visual sensors and then with technology. It is also typical for any species to, at first, imagine that there are other creatures on those planets. Depending on the nature of the species in question, they start out believing one of two things: that the creatures are just like themselves or that they are comparative monsters.

Humans had a brief flirtation with the idea that Martians were living on the fourth planet in their solar system, before they conclusively proved otherwise.

Which is the next inevitable thing. Once again, if time passes and the species still doesn't manage to kill themselves off, it is inevitable that they develop the technology to go visit the other planets in their solar system. If the species has prospects for any true intelligence, they send robotic missions before sending themselves to determine what the place is like before setting their own feet or pods or claws down on them.

But eventually, they decide it's time to leave their rock for a variety of reasons, including everything from curiosity to a nervousness that staying only on their home planet puts them in a precarious position for long-term species survival. They are a single point of failure, and one not-too-big asteroid could wipe them out.

One such yet-to-be-named species, who had their origins on and around the fourth planet in their planetary system, set their sights on the third. They had developed quite advanced optical technology and learned that their third planet was uninhabited. Like any good species, they sent robotic missions ahead of themselves to prepare the place for their arrival. But they kept looking around and found other planets and moons outside their solar system. Which is the third major inevitable practice of species who survive long enough—they start exploring the galaxy.

This species was overly concerned with their own survival and less interested in whether or not there were other species around. Consequently, they began to transform any celestial body within reach that was even slightly suitable for their needs.

Eventually, they decided that the most interesting celestial bodies were around other stars quite far from their own, so they abandoned what they had started in their home system, leaving the robots they put in place on the third planet to fend for themselves.

And fend they did...

Chapter 1

> Ruby <

"For the last time, Uncle Blake, it's okay that you're not going with us," Ruby Palmer said standing with hands on her hips in the most confident pose she could muster. A pose that was meant to say, 'I'm the only human to have left our solar system and single-handedly saved a species of robots, so I'm totally fine on my own.'

On the screen in front of her was her Uncle Blake—a father figure and legal guardian since she was five years old—with his own arms crossed in front of his chest in the most confident and fatherly pose he knew how to make. A pose that said, 'Your galactic escapades gave me a thousand mini heart attacks, so, of course, I'm going to worry.' Because, of course, no matter how many historical events Ruby was a part of, her substitute father slash uncle would always worry, as fathers and uncles do.

He sighed and uncrossed his arms, unfolded them, and they came to rest mostly out of view since the screen cut off at mid-chest.

"Only because you made the choice for me," Uncle Blake said.

Ruby blushed. She was indeed guilty of asking Milo Jenkins, her friend, and fellow mini-R-pod pilot, to bring her and the robots onto SD's ship without being entirely truthful as to why. Milo also hadn't questioned her flimsy story. When it came to Milo, if Ruby said jump, Milo would skip the part where a clear-headed individual might ask several clarifying questions and would instead rush into figuring out how he might invent shoes that could take her to the moon. Of course, Milo agreed. Ruby said she wanted a certain amount of privacy which wasn't possible on Astroll 2—the space station where Ruby had lived since the age of 10. Now that Ruby Palmer was the ultimate celebrity, Astroll 2 had become crowded to nearly its capacity with starstruck tourists and eager entrepreneurs who either hoped her celebrity would rub off on them or saw nothing but dollar signs when they looked at her.

It was indeed a flimsy story since Ruby could have guaranteed privacy in her quarters, and Milo knew it.

The truth was, Detailed Historian, known as Disto, had recently discovered that the robots had used the junk DNA of several species of Earth-based plant life to store quite a bit of historical data on the robots. The robots, Disto in particular, had been looking for this data as part of the Special Project Storage Problem, or *Gorp-Gorp*, as it was known in the Special Projects Branch. That data hunt had led to Ruby getting captured by Swell Driver, known as SD, in the first place, since the robots computed that it was extremely likely that human DNA was the solution to where their data was kept. Apparently, they computed the correct planet, but the wrong species.

Once they figured this out, a vast record of historical information was unleashed upon the generally agitated yet remarkable robots. Within these historical records was information about the origin of the robots and Location Zero—an origin story that started not on Location Zero, but on another planet in Location Zero's planetary system. This planet was located in what the robots knew as a Keep-Out Zone. Given the name, they had always kept out. Especially robots like SD that were tasked with interplanetary and interstellar travel.

"Can I assume that you're headed to that restricted zone?" Uncle Blake asked over the video chatting system.

"It is called a Keep-Out Zone, and you are correct," said SD, who was also in view of the camera next to Ruby. "I have configured the navigation systems so that the ship will not automatically avoid the KOZ. The ship produced complaints at first but now seems to understand our mission. I think."

Uncle Blake looked as if he had a hundred more questions to ask SD, but instead, his face on the screen turned back to Ruby. "You brought food? And the vitamins you're supposed to be taking?"

"Yes," Ruby replied. "It's all back there." She pointed her thumb over her shoulder at a pile of storage bins that were sitting in the corner, strapped to the wall. "We talked about it, and we'll only be gone a week, maybe ten days before they bring me back. I have enough for twenty. Right guys?"

Ruby knew that she could call the group of robots 'guys,' and they understood the idiom—but only because she had explained it several times to them. In great length and with more detail and nuance than Ruby thought was possible for such a simple word. Disto had suggested that if she was ever referring to a group of robots that way that she simply use the word, 'robots' but something about the two-syllable label for a group didn't roll off the tongue as naturally as 'guys,' so, 'guys' it was.

"Yes," Disto responded on behalf of the robots. "We will visit the planet in the KOZ. Based on the data I was able to extract, we should find the beings who created Location Zero and all the robots we know. They are more than that, though. These beings are actively involved in Location Zero's operation and potential…"

He trailed off, and Ruby could see that he was still having a hard time processing what he'd learned.

"You mean the potential reset?" Ruby said, finishing his thought.

"Yes," Disto said. Even though Disto wasn't the kind of robot who could deflate like Ambitious Technician, Ruby would have sworn she saw him deflate a little.

After studying the data he'd found, Disto also learned that there was a built-in event designated for Location Zero which sounded like a reset or upgrade time. The nature of the event was ambiguous, and it wasn't clear which was the more accurate description—reset or upgrade or both. Regardless of the imprecise labeling, Location Zero had a built-in planned upgrade that had the potential to completely reset the planet and every robot associated with it. It appeared that the creators of Location Zero, situated in the KOZ, were in the process of uploading a large software patch and once the upload was complete, would force a reset of the whole planet.

"I wish you would have taken me, or someone with more experience with exoplanets or extraterrestrials," Uncle Blake said.

That made Ruby laugh. "Uncle Blake! Remember who you're talking to? Ruby Palmer. First human to make contact with an alien race." She was mocking the celebrity she had gained but also knew that she wasn't entirely wrong. Exoplanet research had stopped a long time ago and was only done in secret by people like Uncle Blake and a few others. It really wasn't even exoplanet research—it was research on the other worlds in their own solar system, like Titan. She still had plans to get there someday, but lately there always seemed to be something in the present that demanded her attention. Not that she minded—she had grown quite fond of the adventures with her robot friends.

In the meantime, she had let Uncle Blake core dump all the data he could on exoplanets, going as far back as the year 1992 with the first confirmed exoplanet detection. Her MoDaC was full of new information for her to read and study, though data dumps like this could be rather tedious to go through, for once, she was interested. She might have even described herself as more than interested—riveted, even. Ruby skimmed it all while SD was getting ready to leave Astroll 2. Between what she had read about Titan, and about exoplanets and what Disto told her about the planet they expected to find in the KOZ, they were all full of methane.

She concluded that the galaxy was a stinky place.

"Besides me being *the most* qualified human," she continued to her uncle, "the robots wanted me along."

Blake's re-crossed his arms. "Did you say goodbye to Uncle Logan? To Sebastian?"

Ruby pressed her hands into her eyes. "Argh," she said. And then to Disto, "Can I have Milo come back and bring me back to Astroll 2 once more before we take off?"

Ruby could tell that Disto wasn't happy. She could tell he was anxious to get underway. She always knew he wasn't about to say 'no' to her for anything she asked.

"Of course," Disto responded. "But we're staying here on SD's ship."

The robots had confided to Ruby that their experiences with other humans were—Ruby had watched Disto as he seemed to internally scroll through a series of words to find the best one—overwhelming, he had said. They claimed to enjoy their time with Ruby's family, but in general, humans were not their favorite species—except Ruby, who had taken the time to understand how to communicate effectively with them—even though it started out while she was under a wee bit of duress and had no choice—and had been able to help them with their problems. Not knowing exactly what to expect in the KOZ was their next problem, and while much was uncertain, they made it clear to Ruby that they wanted her there by their side as they figured it out.

Chapter 2

> Detailed Historian <

Determined. It was a word Disto ruminated on. He had a purpose, and it was in the process of getting fulfilled. This meant he was satisfied; he was content.

Swell Driver informed him that his ship was ready to depart.

"Let's go, Ruby!" Disto called into the communications line he had opened with Ruby. He still possessed his very own communicuff and could contact her even if she was back on Astroll 2 and he was waiting impatiently in SD's ship.

It was a video comm link, and Disto watched as Ruby stood outside a mini-R-pod with her Uncle Blake, Uncle Logan, and mini-human cousin, Sebastian. Disto knew Milo was waiting inside the mini-R-pod called *Pecan Pi*.

Milo and SD had already made several trips to and from his ship to get it ready. This was one extra trip that he couldn't say no to Ruby making, even though she had seemed to be ready to depart earlier.

There had been a touch of deception, on the part of the humanoid biological beings—the Bios. Ruby's Uncle Blake was the source. He came up with a cover story: Ruby was escorting the robots home, and SD would bring her back.

If the other Bios knew what they were doing, they would have insisted on sending others. They had already insisted on sending other Bios to Location Zero, but Disto was able to convince them that a proper diplomatic situation needed to be established first. Humans should and could prepare for a visit, but they needed to pack their appropriate food and supplies, and robots at Location Zero would prepare quarters in advance.

The arranged time was when the human diplomatic and research team would be picked up from Earth. The biggest difficulty was in agreeing on an adequate level of security for the chosen team.

What the Bios didn't know is that the arranged time was after the upcoming 'reset,' so Disto only hoped that there would still be a Location Zero to visit. Well, there would be. The Reset wouldn't remove or destroy the planet, but he hoped it would be *his* Location Zero, and not some foreign, screwed-up version of it.

A question had been posed: should 'Ruby of the Robots' be allowed to return? But it was clear that no one could tell her no. Rather, she could certainly be told no, but no one expected her to willingly accede to that request. And anyway, the robots wanted her with them, since Disto was certain they would undoubtedly encounter other Bios on the new planet. Ruby's ability to adapt and communicate could only be of help to them. To Disto, it made perfect sense, but Ruby's presence was essential.

"Ruby!" Disto called out again. "SD has informed me that the ship is in a state that is ready for departure."

Ruby held up a single finger. Single. One. But one what?

Disto watched them all embrace on the video link. Then Ruby embraced Sebastian. And then Uncle Blake once more. A few other humans were present, but Ruby didn't embrace them. Instead, they touched hands briefly. Robt Plampton, the Astroll 2 station director, was there. Plampton was one of the few Bios Disto wished he had a little more time to get to know. But once they found out about The Reset, they needed to hurry.

While still on Earth, returning to SD's ship was a mini-adventure unto itself. It took nearly a full week to arrange and complete the journey that involved traveling around half the planet before ascending up the space elevator to Legacy Station. But once on SD's ship, the group was back at Astroll 2 in an appendage full of tics, or a "handful of seconds," as Ruby had said. Ruby had also remarked that they'd been here for too many clicks already—she was also eager to move on.

Ruby was finally inside *Pecan Pi* and Milo closed the hatch.

"Just making up for the fact that the last time I left, I didn't say goodbye properly," she said.

"Indeed," Disto said. Over the comm link, he heard what he could only assume were two Bios positioning themselves into the small, but adequate space inside *Pecan Pi*. "If I understand the sequence of events, you bypassed all of that."

"I left a note," Ruby said at a lower volume.

"Hrmph," was a noise that Disto assumed had to have been made by Milo.

"I thought we agreed we were done talking about the past," Ruby said.

"Maybe your past," added Disto. "But not mine. Not ours. Talking about ours is just beginning…and I just computed that that comment was not directed at me."

"It's okay, Disto. We'll be there in a few moments," Ruby said.

And with that, Disto watched a small ship launch out of Astroll 2 on the large, main viewscreen on SD's ship. One step at a time, he thought.

> Ruby <

In the control center of SD's ship, Ruby felt like she was in a second or third home. She was getting comfortable here. Before they departed, she asked SD if she could pilot the ship herself.

"Unfortunately, you don't have the right access ports to interface with the ship," he had said.

Then Ruby looked on as SD pulled out an appendage and connected it to the console. He interfaced with the ship in a variety of ways. One way, touching the console, was familiar, like how she interfaced with her mini-R-pod. But a direct connection via an appendage—while she could admit might have its efficiencies—was not something she ever hoped would be familiar to her.

Although she was getting closer and closer to having more direct connections herself. Before she left Earth, she let herself be convinced into taking a pair of Percepto-glasses with her. She could never have afforded the really nice ones on her own, but her celebrity status meant that everyone was offering her everything in order for them to get her seal of approval and endorsement. She had refused 80 percent of the stuff she was offered but let herself take a digitally hand-drawn portrait that made her really look nice, a green, fitted jacket with an excess of pockets, and a deck of cards with her face on each that she passed off to her grandmother.

She had gotten in one more visit with her grandmother, Pearl Palmer, before she left Earth as well.

"I'm going to make a killing at my next poker game with this," Pearl had said as they exchanged gifts. Ruby could easily imagine this woman taking everyone's money, with or without cards with her face on them.

Ruby kept the keepsakes her grandmother gave her but didn't bring any of it with her to Location Zero, particularly the jewelry.

But Ruby digitally scanned her mother's journals. It was too impractical to haul all of that mass back to Astroll 2, even if they were going to do it from SD's ship. There was still the problem of getting that mass to the ship.

"I'm sorry, mom," Ruby said to no one, "but this is the safest way I can keep these." She used a fancy scanner, which did it in no time. Then she double encrypted everything so that it would only open with the password she knew and her fingerprint. She put it on her MoDaC.

The MoDaC was tied into the Percepto-glasses, so she didn't need to open the MoDaC anymore except for deep work. It took a little bit to get used to, but Ruby was enjoying this mix of old and new tech.

Pippa didn't like that Ruby had taken on another device. That was until Ruby explained that there wasn't another AI in the glasses, and she could connect Pippa to it as well. That cheered Pippa up.

"So, SD, when will we get there?"

"Momentarily," SD responded.

"I presume we're going to enter as planned…?" Disto asked.

Ruby could now do a few things on SD's ship, and she touched a part of the console that allowed her to turn on the viewscreen and display information on it like a monitor. The approach trajectory for the robots' home planetary system was already set up and programmed in.

There was a star, and orbiting around was Location Zero, in a near perfect, circular orbit. The Keep-Out Zone remained visible on this map, indicated by a dotted line. The KOZ was in the same orbit as Location Zero but on the opposite side of their host star.

SD had described it simply as a place that he was not allowed to take his ship but trailed off every time he said something like that. When Ruby had tried to probe for more, he got even quieter.

Another dotted line was overlaid and in a different color. "There," Ruby said. "Exactly like we talked about. We're going to come in over your planetary system along the spin axis of it. We'll find a quiescent point to look at the KOZ from, and then we'll head to the planet there."

They all looked at the screen for a few moments until Ruby spoke again, "And you have no other information on this planet?"

"There was none in the data I found," Disto confirmed. "Only its existence, the fact that it is indeed responsible for my existence, and the fact that it wants to reset my existence…"

Ruby didn't push. This was a sore subject. Rightfully so. No one wanted to be reset or erased. Well, maybe there was a handful who did, but no one she knew.

Soon, a larger circle appeared over the dotted line. It was blinking and moving along it.

"That's us?" Ruby asked.

"Correct," said SD.

"Wow. I'm still… I don't know what to say." On top of everything, these robots could travel faster than light as easily as she could take a few steps across a room. While they refused to give her or humanity that tech, she wondered if the people they'd meet in the KOZ would. Or if they would provide any indication of how Ruby and her kind could catch up and start to learn that tech. Or was it possible that humans were so far behind everyone else in the galaxy?

The blinking circle that indicated their ship quickly marched along the dotted line and then came to a stop.

"We are now located approximately 592 scruples from our star, which is approximately 141 scruples equidistant from the KOZ and Location Zero."

Ruby tried to imagine a *scruple* in her head. It was a unit of measurement that the robots used both for extremely large distances and infinitesimally small distances, but on a logarithmic scale. She couldn't ever quite picture it. She shook her head because having a clear image wasn't all that important. As long as she knew it worked. What was important was the fact that in this moment, she was truly a galactic explorer.

"This is amazing, SD," Ruby said. "What's the rest of the planetary system like?"

SD touched his console and a variety of other dots of various sizes appeared, orbiting the host star. "Those are the other planets within this system," he said.

Ruby saw that Location Zero and KOZ were in the third orbital position around the host star. Two other planets orbited closer into the star. In orbits further off from Location Zero, were four more planets.

"Are the size of those dots relative to the true size?" Ruby asked.

"Correct," SD responded. "Seven planets orbiting our star. Well, 8 now that we know about the planet in the KOZ."

"The outer ones are the big ones, just like our solar system," Ruby said. The fact that there was an unusually large gap between the third and fourth planets didn't go unnoticed.

"That's common among the systems I have traveled to," SD said.

Ruby blinked. "How many planetary systems have you been to, SD?"

"435 unique planetary systems," he said as unremarkably as if he was telling her how many bolts were on his chassis. If he even had bolts—Ruby still didn't know how any of the robots were physically put together.

Ruby shook her head, taking that in. "SD, that's incredible!"

"I am a Driver," was all he said in response.

"You are! What are we waiting for?" Ruby asked. "Let's go!"

"I am attempting to re-compute the trajectory," SD said. "Once again my computer… won't comply."

Disto rolled over to SD's side to look at the computer console with him. He beeped in displeasure.

"The computer says," SD announced, "that it cannot take us to the KOZ. It will not compute a trajectory through a region of unallowed space. I cannot make it change its mind."

"Can you reprogram it?" Ruby asked.

"Ruby, you know I am not a Programmer," SD responded.

"And you know about our built-in rules about reprogramming," added Disto.

"But I thought that only applied to yourselves. Isn't the ship's computer a non-sentient tool?" Ruby probed.

"Indeed. However, we still do not possess the skills to reprogram at will."

"But I do," Ruby said. "Let me in there."

Ruby connected Pippa to the ship's computer since Pippa also had previous experience with the robots' modes and methods. Together, they were able to 'convince' the ship's computer no zone was prohibited within this planetary system. The computer offered a little protest, in the form of what seemed like an endless stream of "are you sure?" messages, but in the end, Ruby and Pippa were sure, so the computer said

"Okay."

Ruby disconnected Pippa and moved out of the way so SD could resume his work.

He communicated with the computer in his native chirps and beeps and after a series of those emanated from him, with the ship beeping back he said:

"There is one more problem I can see before we get there. My ship should not land on a planetary surface."

Ruby recalled the same problem when they had arrived at Earth. There, they were able to connect to Legacy Station and get down from there. But he just said…

"Wait, you just said 'should not' instead of cannot? Does that mean you can land?" Ruby asked.

SD let out a low beep indicating he was thinking over her question.

"It is not so much the landing as it is the taking off again," SD said. "I can break the link with gravity, but it isn't always predictable."

Ruby did not know how to process what SD said. 'Break the link with gravity' was a phrase she'd never heard before, and she wasn't sure all the PhDs in Physics could help her make sense of that. Problems for later.

"Let's go. Let's get into orbit and have a good look at the place and then figure that out. Agreed?"

"Agreed," SD and Disto said in unison.

The ship resumed movement, and Ruby would have sworn that they were deliberately going slower than necessary. Like the robots wanted to find out what was there and yet they didn't. She understood the feeling of both wanting to know a thing and yet not wanting to know that same thing at the same time.

"When we get there, put us in standard orbit," Ruby suggested.

"What is standard orbit?"

"I don't know. I just said it. It's what they always said in the old vids."

"Ah, yes!" Disto said. "We watched those vids. 'Standard

orbit, ensign.' 'Plot a standard orbit.' Yet they were never specific as to what standard orbit was."

"Yeah, so I know that wasn't helpful. It was fun to say, though." Ruby said, smiling.

"Our approach will take us into a highly eccentric orbit and then lower the... the..." SD was struggling with a translation.

"Apog— Sorry, I mean apoapsis. I almost said the wrong word," Ruby said, "We call the highest point in the orbit the apoapsis. If we're orbiting Earth, we call it the apogee."

"Why is it a different word if you're around Earth?" Disto asked.

Ruby shook her head, "I don't know. It just is," she said. "I think a long time ago, everything was naturally Earth-centric, but over time as people were able to understand there was more beyond Earth, they changed words to accommodate that."

"Sounds inefficient," Disto said.

"It probably is," Ruby said. "At least, it's a lot more to remember. But we gain knowledge a little at a time and have to adapt along the way, so it's sort of the way of things. Anyway. Apoapsis."

"Yes," SD said, "Each orbit the apoapsis will lower until we achieve a low, circular orbit. We will continuously scan the planet looking for... Disto, what are we looking for?"

"Bios," Disto answered. "The ones who created us and who think they have a right to control us now."

> Swell Driver <

Swell Driver was an excellent driver of his ship. He had traveled to many planetary systems and, along with his computer, calculated trajectories through and around systems and planets, using the gravity of massive bodies to slingshot around, going high, going low, and all manner of maneuvers in between.

This trip should have been no different than any of the others.

Yet somehow, something felt oddly familiar about this approach.

Ruby had asked to have the planet in the KOZ displayed in the viewscreen. He complied, yet in doing so, he felt… something. He didn't have all the names for all the feelings he felt in recent times. Every time he seemed to grasp his set of feelings, new ones would enter and he'd lose himself in them again. So—for efficiency's sake alone—he lumped it together with other uncomfortable feelings and tried to concentrate on the job at hand: achieving orbit around this planet.

A part of him wanted to turn the ship around and head for Location Zero, where he could dock his ship and then… what? Revisit the Rejuvenation Region? Take another break from being a Driver? Maybe he wanted to implement one of Explosive Healer's suggestions to externally record all the things he could remember experiencing. "That's journaling," Ruby had said when he mentioned the idea to her. "Just like my mom did."

With all this uncertainty, he kept on course, with Ruby and Disto looking at the planet as they got closer.

"That planet has an atmosphere," Ruby announced, pointing her arm toward the screen.

"That is correct," SD confirmed. "I will have the computer perform a scan analysis of the composition and…"

"What is it?"

"I'm detecting a signal. In fact, I am detecting several signals."

"You are?"

"Correction. My ship's computer is detecting several signals and—and it is not happy."

SD wasn't happy either, but he could clearly attribute this to the interaction between these signals and his ship. One particular signal was establishing its own communication connection with his ship.

SD tried to tell the ship to ignore the communication attempt.

"I cannot," the ship replied.

"Explain," SD answered in his native tones—a more efficient way of communicating with the ship. Disto would be able to understand and would have to translate to Ruby. SD didn't want to be rude, but time and efficiency could be important here.

"The signal has an override code. I am compelled to listen," the ship said. "It is… it is… altering my trajectory."

"How so?" SD asked. While he asked, he could see the computation in progress. The alteration did not make sense. The new trajectory would have them crash land on the KOZ planet.

"Disregard new trajectory," SD ordered, with increasing frustration. He was not used to his ship listening to someone else over him. It was his ship, after all.

"Cannot comply," came the weak response from the computer. "I am… sorry."

SD continued to poke at the computer to try and return them to their original trajectory. But he was locked out. The signal that came in seemed to know exactly how to talk to his computer to make it comply with its wishes. SD overheard Disto behind him talking to Ruby.

"There's got to be something you can do," Ruby said, her eyes scanning the screen with urgency, "Manual override?"

"I do not know that term," SD said.

"I mean, can you stop the computer from completing any actions and take direct control over the ship yourself."

SD thought about that. He could turn the computer off. He could plug himself in and act as the computer. Yes, maybe.

"Yes, maybe," he said out loud.

"Try now, please!" Ruby said. "That planet is way too big on the screen."

Within one tic SD understood that, one: they were still far enough away that the fact that the planet looked big on the viewscreen was an illusion. He could zoom out to a less disturbing image at any time. Two: that Ruby knew that too, and three: that none of that mattered if he didn't get in control of his ship.

Chapter 3

> Three <

"I think they're going to crash."

Three's circuits whirred as she processed what Rocky said. They were not equipped to handle a crash landing.

Rocky didn't wait for Three's circuits to slow down and process any more. She continued, "It's their trajectory. I'm concerned. They are close, but I don't think they are compensating for our unusual fields. Hence, I think they're going to crash."

"Wasn't that the intent of the transmission?" asked Maker. "They shouldn't be coming here anyway."

"Maker! That's terrible!" said Six-Five. Six-Five then whirred up her rotors and lifted off the ground slightly to emphasize her statement.

It was only a little less than a click earlier that Three had rolled over the hill and down to the valley where the rest of her colleagues were present. As was typical, she didn't head here in a straight line but had to navigate the pockets of goo that were unevenly located on the ground.

Seven-Nine, One-Four, and Three-Eight were present in the valley. Three-Five, who flew in to bring them the most recent information, was bored from waiting and took off into the sky once more. Three saw her drift off over the horizon.

As always, they were gathered around Three-Eight, who was immobile. The others called her "Habby," but Three preferred using everyone's official designation. Habby was equipped with a large inner cavity originally designed to support Bio-life. She was the largest by volume of any of the robots and quite observant. Her optical sensors allowed her to see both inside and out, in all directions and as far as the horizon. And while her insides were designed for Bio support, she was still useful for repairing her smaller companions like Three-Eight or Six-Five, who rarely returned to base.

It was odd that Seven-Nine and One-Four were perched so close together. Well, Seven-Nine had no choice in the matter. She was perched close to Habby, and as the source of power for Habby and the other fixed robots, stayed put. It was One-Four that must have approached her. One-Four had her own power cells that, like any of them who were mobile, could collect enough energy from their Sun, so they rarely had to visit Seven-Nine. Most of the others didn't have patience for Seven-Nine. This was fine with Seven-Nine who preferred to be left alone with her thoughts anyway.

Three, however, was usually the one to seek out Seven-Nine's counsel. Three appreciated how Seven-Nine always relied on logic and reason and Seven-Nine's desire to learn about everything enabled her to sift through information, combating bias and misinformation. Like when they first arrived, and their operations began on this planet. Seven-Nine kept in constant communication with all the mobile robots, collecting their data as they effortlessly and continuously sampled the rock and the goo and the atmosphere. It was a shame she wasn't mobile, but her connectivity to the other parts of the base gave her access to all the same information they all had. So, Seven-Nine would set herself to any computation task that wasn't boring or menial.

Heck, generating power for her companions wasn't menial either, but relied on constantly monitoring the rod buried deep inside her. The rod was stuck under layers and layers of dense, silver metal. Three appreciated the fact that out of every one of the robots on this planet, Seven-Nine was the one with the most important job, and thusly was relied upon by everyone who couldn't get all their energy from their sun.

So, it was interesting that One-Four was nearby. Although the fact that she attempted to trail along wherever Three went wasn't all that interesting. It's that she usually didn't come on a visit to Seven-Nine. While One-Four generally preferred the company of others, she often did not enjoy the company of Seven-Nine.

One-Five, also known as Rocky, and Three-Two, also known as Maker, were installed nearby because of course they were—both permanently positioned near Habby, so they were always close enough to listen in on communications and have their say.

Four-Six and Six-Five rarely met with the others. Four-Six enjoyed roaming the landscape as much as she could, and Six-Five could barely ever stay still. The second Six-Five would land, she'd be taking off again. The only thing that brought her to the ground was the need to soak up additional power from Seven-Nine on days that their sun wasn't enough. At the moment, Six-Five decided to ground herself nearer to Seven-Nine and One-Four.

"Don't get too comfortable," said One-Four. Three wanted to comment on One-Four's condescension, but now wasn't the time.

Three had perched herself in the center of her companions, turning around in the smallest circle her wheels would allow her to make in order to get everyone's attention.

"We're about to have visitors," she said. "Unplanned visitors. One-Five, do we have an idea of where their trajectory will put them?"

"First and for the last time, call me Rocky," One-Five, or rather, Rocky, said. "We've been over this more than a thousand times. It's easy to replace my formal designator with the alias."

Three's circuits whirred. Why didn't her companions understand her need to use official designations? They were, after all, here to execute their programming. They were not here to simply lounge around and waste time disclosing self-identifiers.

"I will need a little more time to compute the precise position of where they will crash land," said Rocky.

"And Three-Two, remember that we were attempting to direct the ship to land, not crash," said Three. "Can we warn them? Rocky?"

"Negative. Well, not unless you want Eight-Nine to pause her current activity. She will finish shortly, but not in time to help the visitors."

Three allowed her circuits to compute other possibilities. While she loved a challenge, she did not like accepting that they couldn't achieve any goal, big or small. When none of her computations yielded a better result, she rolled back and pointed upwards so her sensors could get a better look at the sky.

"We always knew this was a possibility," she said.

"We'll be able to repair Swell Driver if he's damaged. And his ship," said Rocky. "There should be two other robots with him unless they stayed in the Bio system. The information we received from the sentinel on Location Zero confirmed that a total of three robots escorted the Bio home. Presumably, they found the additional data that we had stored in the DNA of biological species—information that discloses our existence—and that's why they are on their way here."

"It's logical that all three robots would come," Seven-Nine, who made her first contribution to the conversation. Three turned in her direction.

"Yes, I agree," Three said. "Especially Detailed Historian. His mission has been, essentially, to find us. The robots never intended to construct their own missions like that. Once Eight-Nine has finished transmitting the updated code, we can have her send The Reset signal, and then Location Zero should be back on track with their original purpose and get back to producing the results we need."

"Do you really think we'll find the Contractors?" Three-

Five said as she lifted off of the ground, her rotors spinning, she started to loop around the others who were all stuck on the ground.

"Nine-Two believed it, so I do, too," said Three. And then to the others, particularly Rocky, who continued to use her computational power to help instead of study rock after rock, "Let's see what we can do to monitor their trajectory and be nearby and available for repairs when they ultimately crash. Remember, when they get here, communicate no words about our mission. If they knew about the updated code and pending reset, they might attempt to stop it."

"Why would they do that?" said Habby.

Three turned towards the large construct. "Habby, if I told you that I was going to upload a new set of programming instructions and then reset you such that you won't remember what your life was like before, how would you react?"

Three waited patiently for Habby to compute an answer.

"Well, there's not much to remember so maybe it wouldn't matter so much. We've sat here for clicks and clicks and clicks doing not much of anything."

Three's circuits got hot. "We've done amazing things! We've kept ourselves functioning and ready for the Contractors to return. We've kept *on mission.* Even after we lost Nine-Two. That all must count for *something.*" She began to roll away, but stopped.

"Then what was the point, Three?"

"The mission. The point is always the mission."

Chapter 4

> Detailed Historian <

Disto polled his sensors. Each of them reported a short quantity of tics with data missing. He computed that he had been offline for nearly 600 tics. His visual sensors were taking too long to return to their operational state, and he was anxious to have a look around. His audio sensors heard… that was AT's voice.

"Ruby? Ruby! Ruby?" AT was repeating.

Disto forced his visuals to bypass their routine check and activated them. They took a moment to adjust to collecting photons from the cabin—they were still in the main control center of SD's ship—before revealing the scene before him.

Ruby Palmer was in one of the chairs that had been installed when they were on Astroll 2, but the chair tore loose from its mount. It was compressed up against one wall. But Ruby was in it, and her eyes were closed. Disto could make out the tell-tale signs of Bio life. Ruby's primary chassis was performing the intake and output of the surrounding gas. She was alive. That was good. But she was unresponsive. That was bad.

Disto moved over to see if he could be of assistance. SD was at the console of his ship, presumably checking on its status.

"You had downloaded human repair manuals?" Disto asked AT.

AT made a noise that indicated, "Yes, but…" With one appendage on Ruby's arm, he said, "Yes, but…"

"But?" Disto prodded.

"But humans are quite complicated. I have a general template manual. Humans require individualized manuals."

"Interesting. You could not find a Ruby Palmer manual?"

"That's what I'm trying to communicate to you. One does not exist!"

"What does the general manual say?"

"There is no information for the scenario of unconsciousness with potential and unknown internal systems failures following a spaceship crash." AT paused, moved his appendage to different locations on her arm and then said, "I can tell you that she is alive. I can detect her inner systems are not stagnant."

"Can you also—"

"Mmmmmpppphhhh…" The noise wasn't a word in her language but definitely came from Ruby.

"Ruby!" Disto and AT said.

Ruby performed the very Bio action of blinking—opening and closing the shutters that protected her optical sensors.

"Don't move," AT said.

Ruby did not heed AT's command. Instead, she used her arms to adjust her position in the chair, so she was sitting in more or less an upright position.

"Are your audio sensors damaged?" AT asked. "I said do not move."

Ruby touched the side of her head, "My audio sensors are fine," she said with a very slight smile. "But there's a ringing…"

AT looked at Disto and said, "In the supplies we brought, there is a human medical repair kit. Can you locate it?"

Disto chirped affirmatively and moved to the lift at the back of the cabin. Before he opened the door, he called out to SD, "Is it functioning?"

Without looking away from what he was doing, SD responded, "Yes. There is significant damage to my ship, including the primary computer. But internal secondaries like the lift should still be functioning."

SD's tone and coloring indicated that SD was a mix of frustrated, sad, and hopeful. But SD's feelings would have to wait. AT needed that medical kit to attend to Ruby.

Thankfully, the lift still worked so in a mere few tics, Disto found himself in front of several large crates of Bio supplies that they had brought with them. He could not immediately locate a manifest, so he started opening crates without the aid of data.

The first one he opened contained a Bio-sized, more specifically, a Ruby-sized suit. They knew that the planet they were headed to did not have an atmosphere compatible with Ruby's atmosphere processing systems, and if they were going to be on the surface, she'd need it. When Disto opened the second crate, he became quite disheartened looking at a pile of smaller, unmarked containers. He picked up one and realized they were marked, but on the side, not the top. He put each aside after confirming that they were foodstuffs. Disto had learned that the food at Location Zero was not entirely good for Ruby. It appeared they brought the nutrients she needed.

Disto worried he was taking far too long and there were still four more crates to examine. But then he emitted one of words that he'd added to his vocabulary while in the lab with several scientists on Earth: "Voila!"

The first container in the third crate was labeled 'medical supplies.' Disto started returning the items he had removed from the second crate back to their original location before computing that that action was a waste of tics right now. He dropped the box labeled 'emergency chocolate' and rushed as fast as he could with the 'medical supplies' back to Ruby and their companions.

When he arrived, he ewas concerned that Ruby was still in the same position as when he left. Ruby was not the type to sit around for long, nor was she the type to listen when others told her she must sit.

"I convinced her to keep her current position until we could determine the extent of her injuries," AT said triumphantly.

"How did you do that?" Disto asked as he turned over the medical kit.

AT beeped. Clearly, he did not want to answer that question. Instead, AT turned his attention to the kit, using his precision appendage to carefully investigate the contents.

"That scanner…" Ruby said. "That's what you want."

While Disto was quite concerned with Ruby's health and status, he was also interested in the beep AT made. "AT?" he prompted.

"Not now. I'm scanning." Indeed, by then he had the scanner aimed at Ruby's body and was moving it up and down, presumably collecting data. When he finished, both AT and Ruby looked at the small screen readout simultaneously.

"Great." Ruby said.

"You're great?" Disto responded, relieved.

"Remember when I tried to explain sarcasm to you?" Ruby said. Disto performed his version of a nod. "That was sarcasm."

"Therefore, you're not great. You are damaged," Disto said.

"I'm bruised. But I could have told you that without the scanner. Nothing more severe than that. But," she performed the very human motion of sighing, "it looks like I have a slight concussion."

"What's a concussion?" Disto asked.

"A mild blow to the head, with or without loss of consciousness, which can lead to temporary impairment of cognitive function and manifest in other cognitive symptoms," AT chimed in. "That's from the information I downloaded."

"Thanks," Ruby said. She was moving now, trying to position herself to stand.

"Wait," Disto said, a little louder than he'd intended, but he did intend for her to stop moving. "Shouldn't AT repair your concussion first?"

Ruby smiled, "I had this once before when I was twelve. Slight incident while playing table tennis. There's nothing AT can do."

Disto looked to AT for confirmation.

"Correct. The information I have says it will self-repair with rest and restriction of activities."

Ruby was again trying to stand up, so Disto again blurted out, "Wait!"

"I'm allowed to stand," she smiled as she said it. "The kind of activities they don't want me to do are the ones that could cause another concussion. A small one isn't that bad. Multiple concussions at the same time are."

She stood up and immediately said, "Whoa…" and looked for something to hold on to. "This is not ship's gravity."

SD was the one who responded to Ruby's statement, "That is correct. You are feeling the gravity of the planet, which, putting in terms of your home world, Earth, is approximately 80 percent."

"Just enough to knock me off balance," Ruby said, gripping the chair. "Maybe I will sit down until we figure out what we're doing."

"That depends on the status of the ship," Disto said. "SD? Do you have this information?"

"I do," SD said. And then said no more. After a few tics, Disto asked, "Can you share this information with us?"

"I can," SD said. And then said no more. After a few tics, a frustrated Disto asked, "Would you share your information with us now?"

"Yes," SD said, moving away from the console and facing the rest of them.

"The ship is severely damaged," SD said. Disto wanted to say, 'We knew that' but refrained until he heard what SD was going to say next.

"The ship's computer has indications that components we need to lift off are damaged, as is much of the deep communication…" SD cut himself off and turned his attention to the console. Disto knew that SD had a direct connection to the ship's computer and assumed they were in communication right now.

After a few tics, SD's facescreen refreshed to indicate that he had completed that communication.

"SD?"

"The computer," he began. "I'm sorry. I'm still processing. Processing. The computer has indicated that parts I did not know existed on my ship have been damaged. There is a deep communication system I did not know was present."

As SD made his report, Disto watched AT's excitement build. He clearly wanted to start repairs immediately.

"What's outside?" Disto and Ruby asked simultaneously. Simultaneous emissions such as those were rare and Disto almost distracted himself by wanting to mark the occasion. A glance from Ruby told him she might have had a similar thought that didn't get expressed because SD answered the question.

"I think the source of the transmission we picked up is nearby," SD said.

"Ooo! We should go check it out! I'll need to get my suit!" said Ruby and she moved past him, a little too fast for someone recently injured.

SD was involved with his ship, Ruby was prepping to head outside, and AT was figuring out which tools he could use to effect repairs. Disto had nothing to do but wait and count down the tics until The Reset.

Chapter 5

> Ruby <

"You look… engorged," Disto said.

"Swollen is how I would have described it," AT added.

Ruby looked down at the parts of her body she could see. SD's ship didn't have a mirror, so she was unable to see the full effect of how she presented to the robots in this thing. It was somewhere halfway between comfortable, like sleepwear, and utterly uncomfortable, like what ancient space suits were known to be. The outer surface was a light blue, so she must have looked like a series of large, light blue marshmallows smashed together in humanoid form to the robots. The helmet was half opaque and half clear, so when it was on her head, the robots could still see her face and she had her full range of peripheral vision. The suit also allowed her to bend her joints with little effort. The insides of the legs were soft but rigid. The arms were more flexible, but less soft. It seemed that wherever comfort was, discomfort made room for itself.

She hadn't donned an Intelli-Gear suit since she had to practice emergency ops with one. Pilots were required to be retrained yearly, and it was nearly a year since she'd last worn it.

However, she was able to successfully connect her communicuff to the suit's systems so she could activate Pippa by voice only and she would see projected visuals that appeared to her as if they were several feet in front of her. It was very similar technology to her Percepto-glasses, but in suit form.

"Pippa," she said, "suit check."

There was no holoimage of Pippa. Ruby asked Pippa to keep that kind of unnecessary visual to a minimum, but added in a compliment about the personalized image Pippa was fond of projecting. It wasn't that Ruby didn't like it. She needed to see as much as possible of this new world without anything blocking her vision—no matter how translucent the images and data were. She was already prepared for new levels of overstimulation, and with her new concussion to keep an eye on, she couldn't be too careful.

A list of suit systems appeared in front of Ruby. The display wasn't on the screen in her helmet, right next to her face, but rather a reality augment that appeared from her perspective to be several feet in front of her, almost next to Disto. Not that he or anyone but Ruby could see it.

"Oxygen pack one all good," Pippa announced. As she did, the corresponding word was highlighted in the list for Ruby to see and correlate. Pippa listed all the systems one by one: Primary life support, back-up life support, tertiary life support… since the suit was all about life support, really.

"Dismiss," Ruby commanded, and her view cleared. She could call up the status at any time with a simple command.

She opened and closed her hands several times ensuring she had a full range of movement for each of her fingers. The suit was a little stiff, but it was the stiffness of a suit that was brand new, never worn.

She also took a few steps back and forth and bent down to make sure her knees, ankles and everything could move. When she was satisfied, she put her hands on her hips and said:

"Okay, I'm ready to head outside!"

She knew she was swaying a little as she said it. 80 percent gravity should have been easy for her, but was not feeling 100 percent steady on her feet, so she inched herself back until she was leaning against the bulkhead. Still, swaying didn't deter her confidence. She clenched her fist as much as the suit's glove would let her, narrowed her eyes through the visor, and readied herself for whatever this new world had to throw at her.

SD commanded the ship to open the hatch. The outside air rushed in and mingled with the inside air. Ruby remembered that she never got a satisfactory answer to why the air on SD's ship, and Location Zero, was already a breathable and non-toxic mix. She hoped that she could assume it could return it to that state later. But those issues would need to wait.

They were here, and the swirl of air that rushed in was… warm. A cozy kind of warm. Like gentle humid air that wants to hang around and be friends instead of breezing past. The Intelli-Gear was designed to allow the wearer to experience as much of the ambient environment as possible. Once that environment started to go out of range to support life, systems would kick in. The wearer could choose to make it warmer, or cooler based on personal preference as well.

"Pippa," Ruby said. "Atmosphere readout." While she trusted SD and his ship—at least in the sense that she trusted that SD would not intentionally mislead or lie to her—she wasn't sure she could trust that his equipment was working or that it was designed to pick up what was important to humans.

Once again, the Intelli-Gear displayed a set of data to her, and Pippa simultaneously read it.

"Primary atmosphere constituents are nitrogen and methane at a ratio of 17 to 3," Pippa paused, "That's very close to the atmosphere of Titan. Radiation levels are high. We're detecting nearly a centi-rem."

Ruby had to remember that 'we' meant Pippa and the suit.

"Then that means I'm going to need to keep this suit on and let it filter out the methane. Got it."

She might have been able to tolerate the methane, but not the radiation. Luckily, the suit, like most materials made to operate in space, had a thin layer of protective metallic that generated enough of a magnetic field to deflect incoming cosmic rays and other damaging protons, but didn't interfere with standard electronics. This thin layer was built into everything—all ships, most personal clothing, and even standard coffee containers offered that kind of protection.

"Temperature is 26 degrees Celsius; Ambient humidity is

roughly 95 percent."

"No wonder it's so warm," Ruby said. "But wait, is there water in the air, Pippa?" Ruby flexed her fingers and closed them repeatedly. The suit still felt stiff.

"Ruby," Disto interrupted. "It sounds like you are talking to yourself."

"I'm talking to Pippa, and she's talking back to me through the speakers in the helmet. Argh. Pippa, the robots want to hear what you're saying as well. Turn on the external speakers."

"Testing, testing," said Pippa.

"You're performing tests?" Disto asked. "What kind?"

"I was testing my ability to communicate with you," Pippa responded. "I would say the test was successful."

"Okay," Ruby said, "*Now,* can we all go outside?"

Chapter 6

> Ruby <

Ruby was the first one to step outside of the ship. Even though she had already been on an alien world, Location Zero, this was something else entirely. As she stepped out onto the strange regolith of the new planet, it crunched beneath her feet like dry breakfast cereal. She'd never been to the Moon or Mars, but the texture of the ground felt and looked like what she imagined both of those places to be like, although instead of gray or a burnt orange commonly associated with Mars, the dominant color here was a yellowish green. The sky also had a yellowish and greenish haze to it. Perhaps it was the concussion, but it was making Ruby a little queasy. While yellows and greens weren't her favorite colors, if it wasn't for the queasiness, Ruby might have found it pretty. It was daytime, but the sky was hazy enough that she couldn't immediately locate the direction of the host star.

"Pippa, am I getting ambient audio?" she asked. It was quiet. Too quiet. Although that shouldn't have surprised her too much. There wasn't anything around to make noise other than her, and the robots—who were starting to leave SD's ship, with Disto in front and SD in the back.

"Yes," Pippa responded.

When Ruby was about three meters from the ship, she stopped and slowly turned around to one: take in the full effect of the landscape, and two: get a good look at the ship. The outside didn't look too beat up, but it was partially sitting in a patch of… *goo?* Goo didn't feel like a very scientific term, but it was the only word popping into Ruby's head as she stared at the slow moving, translucent, gobbildy-gook that partly encased the bottom of the ship. As she looked around, she saw varying sizes of poppy yellow or orangish yellow goo on the ground.

Once again, she was reminded of images she had seen of Mars. In fact, if it wasn't for the background color, if you told her she was on Mars, she would have believed you. Except she didn't recall ever seeing or hearing about goo on Mars. So then again, she probably wouldn't have believed it, until she took a closer look at the puddles of slime.

There were hills in the distance and Ruby instantly wondered if they'd landed in a crater. There was no way for her to know right now. The hills looked rough and rocky. There was nothing that could be considered vegetation in sight, hence the comparison to Mars or even the Moon. As she continued to turn, taking in the whole scene, the hills seemed to only surround them halfway. The other half was flatter terrain than she'd ever seen. Again, not a sign of anything that looked like vegetation. Also, no buildings or ruins or any signs of any people or any habitation.

"We need to decide how we're going to talk about direction here," Ruby announced.

"That's the equivalent of North," SD chimed in. He had been so quiet and motionless, but now he was pointing towards the middle of the hills. "And that's East," he was now pointing 90 degrees to the right of the hills.

The other two robots and Ruby all looked at him quizzically, but none of them said what Ruby was thinking, and what she was sure the other robots were thinking, *How did he know that?* But Ruby wasn't satisfied not knowing the answer to that question, so she came up with one on her own: *He has been here before. Maybe not on the surface, but in orbit. There must be some form of magnetosphere to orient north and south, and spin, to orient east and west. It's that simple.* And it was that simple, except for the part where SD must have been here before and no one else knew about this place. No, there was nothing simple about this.

"Pippa," Ruby said, "Do you detect any magnetosphere? Can you anchor that direction as North?" Ruby pointed in the direction SD had indicated.

"Affirmative," Pippa replied. "We have calibrated our compass. But our direction module was not meant for exploring new worlds."

"Well, Pippa, sometimes we all have to operate out of our comfort zones," Ruby said. She was indeed outside of her comfort zone, but no… she wasn't. She was more uncomfortable being too comfortable. At home, she was restless. This was exciting. This was *her*. She was exploring a new world. A new alien world that no human had ever set foot on. She knelt onto the ground and felt the terrain through her suit gloves, crumbling small rocks into dust. Something about this made her smile and wonder how she could feel so at home somewhere so far from home. She looked out at the flat emptiness and imagined all that could be beyond it, unable to keep herself from feeling that this may be exactly what she was meant to do with her life. Not continue to build out a colony on an existing world like Titan but be one of the first to set foot on new places. Of course, that option had never occurred to her before since human spaceflight was limited to her home solar system. All the places that humans could step down on comfortably, with the aid of a space suit, well, humans had. This option had never been available until now.

Maybe when this was done, she could offer to go explore strange new worlds with SD and the other robots? Assuming they could fix SD's ship and get off this world. And assuming that they could find the source of the pending software reset to prevent the robots from turning into who knows what. Or at least prevent their memories and existing personalities from being erased.

"We should probably inspect your ship, SD," Ruby said. Then she noticed that was exactly what AT was doing. He hadn't marveled at the landscape like she had, or stared longingly into the distance looking for something, like Disto.

AT was in the process of a methodical circumnavigation of SD's ship. Ruby took several steps to catch up to him. She heard each one of her steps make a crunching sound in the alien regolith as she did so. This was the closest she'd ever come to the outside of SD's ship. It looked… smooth. She didn't dare touch the outside not knowing if it was still hot from entering the atmosphere, or if there was a lot of electrical charge build up, or something she hadn't thought of. *Look, don't touch.* She could hear the voice of her uncles inside her head telling her to be careful. The robots even had to say it 100 times the day they brought her to the Museum of Intricate Specimens on Location Zero, but right now, that seemed like useful survival advice.

"I commend your driving skills, Swell Driver," AT said. SD had also followed Ruby's steps and now the three of them were involved in the inspection. "Or maybe it's your crashing skills I am complimenting. I am not detecting any damage to the primary structure. This was a very well executed crash."

SD chirped what Ruby recognized as 'thank you.'

"How are we going to launch it back into orbit?" Ruby asked.

"That's a later problem," Disto said. Disto had been so quiet, for a moment, Ruby thought he had gone back inside the ship.

"I don't know, seems like a now *and* later problem to me. I know you all have advanced technology, but last time we talked about SD's ship landing and launching, back at Earth, it didn't seem like SD's ship was built for this."

"I never said the ship couldn't land on Earth," SD said.

Both Disto and Ruby turned to him, both wearing an expression that said, 'explain more!'

"My ship is designed to land and take off from any celestial body less than 141 densitons."

"Wait a minute," said Ruby, "Then why did we go through all that with Legacy Station?" She recalled how they chose to dock with the station when they arrived at Earth, causing an electrostatic incident, damage to their equipment, and additional headaches.

"I didn't want to get my ship dirty," SD said.

Luckily, there was enough room in the Intelli-Gear suit for Ruby's jaw to drop and it did. She also knew that his ship was now quite dirty in a pile of goo. That was the definition of irony, right?

Ruby took a deep breath and said, "Okay, forget about that. Let's deal with the problems at hand."

"Indeed," Disto said. "And I think we have new problems to add to the list."

"Oh?" Ruby put her hands on her hips, "And what's the new one?"

Disto pointed in a direction she hadn't spent much time looking at yet, south.

"That," he said.

North, with the hills, was more interesting to look at. When Ruby turned south, all she could discern was a large, flat plain. At least at first. Now, on her second look, she saw what looked like a vehicle. It was moving. And it was heading in their direction.

Chapter 7

> Four-Six <

"Are you seeing what I'm seeing?" Four-Six asked. Four-Six wasn't sure exactly who she was asking and didn't care if it was Three-Five or Three herself who answered.

Four distinct objects were positioned outside of the ship, perched awkwardly on the ground. Three of the objects were clearly robots from Location Zero and they were obviously from at least two different sectors.

But the fourth object… it was a very odd-looking robot. It did not have a ground chassis but balanced oddly on two—wait—Four-Six had seen this before. This was in her design specifications, something she hadn't needed to think about in a long time. It's exactly what her belly was designed for: a Bio.

Four-Six hadn't been at the meeting with the others. Whenever they all got together, which was infrequent, someone was always yelling at someone else. Or, if they promised no one would yell—which they often did for her sake—conflict would still escalate in a more passive-aggressive manner, which was still stressful to Four-Six. She preferred to roam about the terrain, pushing her limits further and further. She was indeed limited by the amount of power before a recharge was necessary, but out of all her companions who were mobile she was the one with the furthest range.

Which is why she was the one chosen to greet the…

intruders? Strangers? There was an argument over what to call them and she was glad she wasn't present for that. Instead, she started heading in their direction before she was fully debriefed.

Four-Six decided all on her own she would simply call them 'visitors.'

Like her companions, she knew much of their own backstory and history. Four-Six and her companions were confined to this world, abandoned by their own creators—well, not entirely abandoned. The Contractors simply no longer existed, but their programming could not accept that, and they needed the Contractors back.

Four-Six still maintained a record of the day of the Big Decision.

"We have everything we need," Nine-Two had said. "There are objects in orbit that we control. We will relocate them to collect supplies. We will build a computational system. It will be as large as a small planet. It will be our exploration system."

Four-Six had a record of Three and the others agreeing and planning. Four-Six herself had a very small role in the whole project but agreed that exploring the surrounding galaxy to find the Contractors was a worthy goal. After all, she was created to host several Contractors at a time in her belly. Without the Contractors, she had very little purpose.

She provided a copy of her core programming to use as a template for robots that they created to live and be a part of Location Zero. Her other ten companions did the same. All the robots on Location Zero were based on one of these eleven templates, at least programming-wise, at least initially. The Location Zero robots didn't have the physical limitations Four-Six and her companions had. But Location Zero was still in beta test and the final version of their programming was nearly ready for execution. Eight-Nine simply needed to finish transmitting it to Location Zero's Core.

Swell Driver was one robot who they programmed more directly, for special tasks. And for some unknown reason, he was on his way to them. They were certain that he was bringing at least one other robot with him. Maybe two. And then they crash landed and now Four-Six, the largest and most mobile of the eleven companions, was on her way to retrieve them.

She hoped they weren't badly damaged. If they were, and if they weren't able to be mobile under their own power, her internal cavity would certainly hold three, maybe more, robots. It was a long time since she carried anything inside, and the thought tickled her. She was thankful that they landed where the terrain was easy, although she had to be mindful of the goop that was scattered around. She could tolerate a little more than her mobile companions, but too much and she'd need a deep clean. But she still preferred this terrain to the hills that were further north and difficult for her to traverse.

Once, a long time ago, she carried the Twins—Three-Five and Six-Five—in her belly to the base of the Hills and let them fly around. The Twins were the only two that could fly. Their range in the air was not as far as hers on the ground and they had been dying to explore the Hills but couldn't get there on their own from the base.

But today, Four-Six traveled alone. Aloneness, she didn't mind. But a visitor could be quite entertaining.

She was only equipped with line-of-sight communication equipment, as were most of her companions, so they set up the usual system when she was on an exploratory mission. Three-Five and Six-Five took positions hovering as high as they could between her and base so they could relay any information back and forth.

"Are you there yet?" Three-Five asked.

"Negative," Four-Six responded. "I had to slow my rate of movement temporarily because the terrain turned rocky."

"How much further? Do I need to fly higher? I can do that you know," Three-Five responded.

Four-Six could tell that her flying companion was incredibly excited. That was when she was willing to take risks. Three-Five was already hovering at the maximum altitude that was deemed safe. But she was always looking for reasons, or excuses, to fly higher.

"Negative. But you should be able to see the crash site and should be able to see how far away I am. It shouldn't be much further."

Four-Six's optical sensors weren't terribly good at distance, but they were keen in the vicinity around her and in front of her. What she could detect at the moment was only a blur, but as she continued on, that blur had come into focus. It was most definitely a ship.

"Three-Five? I assume you see it, too?" Four-Six asked.

"Yes! Yes! I see it! Do you need me to move in closer? Or fly higher?"

"Again, Three-Five. Negative! If you come any closer, I won't be able to communicate back through you and Six-Five to Three. Speaking of which, let them know we have visual detection of Swell Driver's ship. I will be there momentarily."

Four-Six continued to move in the direction of the ship. She had been this far North only a few times before, to scout and map the terrain. And of course, her trip with the twins to the hills. She did another self-systems check to make sure her belly was ready for guests.

As she got closer, she could see more detail but she was no longer interested in the detail of the ship itself, but of the objects that were next to it.

"Image capture on confirmed," she said in a way that indicated Three-Five should relay that back to Six-Five who would relay that back to Three. "Image relay to begin momentarily."

She captured an impression of the scene in front of her. Once she had moved a length or two more, she captured another. These images were now automatically being relayed back to Three who would analyze them along with the others.

"That's definitely a Bio! They have a Bio with them," Four-Six screamed excitedly.

"Are you sure?" Three-Five responded.

"Of course I'm sure! Doesn't anybody but me and Habby remember the Bios?" Habby, what they called Three-Eight, was constructed for similar reasons—to support Bio life in their bellies. To that end, Four-Six always felt a stronger kinship to Habby than any of the others.

"Three confirms," Three-Five said. "They are also saying you need to approach with caution."

"Well of course," Four-Six responded. "What do we know about this Bio?"

There was a pause, while messages were relayed back to Three and data was sent back.

"According to Three," Three-Five said, "the sentinels on Location Zero had recently reported activities on a Bio that Swell Driver had collected and brought there. The Bio was… repairing Core systems? That can't be right. Four-Six, hold on and let me get clarification on that."

Four-Six continued to approach, but slowly. The three robots and one Bio were clearly aware of her by now. They were all stationary and looking in her direction.

A gust of wind passed through, stirring up the dirt and dust. Four-Six grumbled in disapproval as the dust momentarily impaired her vision and interfered with communications. Poor Three-Five seemed particularly affected and she had to lower her altitude, so the signal was barely making it to her.

"Bio… careful…" Static punctuated the signal. "Don't—"

"Don't what?" Four-Six asked but didn't get a response. Static.

"Four-Six? Are you there? Are you okay?"

Of course Four-Six was okay. It was only a little dust interference. It would clear soon, and communication would resume. But what should she do in the meantime? Approach? Stay and do nothing?

Four-Six tried to compute what it might be like if something larger than herself approached her and simply stopped. That would be unpleasant. So maybe the right thing to do was continue on and introduce herself to the visitors? That was the polite thing to do. But she was supposed to not do something and that could have been anything.

Four-Six could feel herself heating up and it was unpleasant. For the moment, she would do absolutely nothing but let her emotions settle down and think of the perfect greeting for when she inevitably approached the visitors. "Hello," simply wasn't going to cut it.

Chapter 8

> Three <

"A Bio!" shouted One-Four as she spun her wheels, kicking up bits of rock and goo.

"Careful!" shouted Three. "But, yes. A Bio. We need to determine if it's the same one Swell Driver had brought to Location Zero. I compute two options. Swell Driver and the others returned the original Bio to its homeworld and brought along another, or this is that same Bio."

"I calculate a higher probability that this is the same Bio," said Rocky.

"Agreed," said Three. Three wished she could have been out there with Four-Six, but she simply didn't have the range. Her mobility was limited, and she moved a lot slower and more deliberately than her mobile companions. She wanted to curse her makers for that, but that would be entirely unhelpful. She needed to purge those thoughts and figure out what to do next. She was, after all, the defacto leader of this group of robots— ever since Nine-Two went missing.

But in any case, it was probably best that Nine-Two wasn't here. Nine-Two was too conservative, too judgmental. One time, Three appeared at a group meeting having recently removed her Bio seats. With no Bios around, she didn't want to carry around the extra weight all day, every day. Three tried to explain that it wasn't energy efficient, but Nine-Two was not happy and let everyone know it. Even now, simply remembering her words of disapproval made Three vibrate unpleasantly.

Three rolled over to Habby. Close enough that the others wouldn't hear.

"Habby, I'd really like to hear your computations on the situation."

Habby opened and shut her main hatch. Matching the ambient atmosphere with that of what she carried in her belly always calmed her down.

"There should be nothing disconcerting about a Bio," she said. "We were created by Bios, for Bios. Bios should be living with us, and in a few cases, inside us. They should be putting us to use. We've been on our own too long. Far too long."

Three considered Habby's words. Habby, formally known as Three-Eight, was right. All of them owed their existence to a group of Bios that was long gone. Who cared that this Bio was not one of them—not one of the Contractors.

"But what if this Bio wants to interfere with our project," said Three-Two, also known as Maker. Maker was usually fond of change but was also fond of contradicting Three.

"I didn't ask you," Three said, "Yet." She rolled over to Maker who was, unsurprisingly, making something at that moment.

"What are you making?" Three asked.

"I accessed my archived data. Old designs for items that I never made because the Contractors never lived here. Maybe this new Bio could use them."

Three rolled back and forth slightly as she watched Maker's systems carefully extract material from the ground with one long appendage. She then used her next long appendage to heat and lay material, one single thin layer at a time on top of another to construct a bio-sized pole sticking out from a base, with appendages protruding from the sides.

"What is that supposed to be?" Three said.

"A welcome gift," Maker responded.

Three resisted the urge not to swirl her optical sensors. "But what *is* it? Its function?"

"It is a device to hold bio-wearables. Remember how the Bios would shed and replace their outermost protective layers? They can use my creation—my own design of course—to temporarily hold them."

Three noticed a slight blemish on the side facing away from Maker but didn't say anything. Maker was not good at handling any kind of criticism, no matter how well-meaning, and right now, Three didn't want to handle anyone not handling anything.

Three rolled back to the center of her stationary colleagues and announced, "We'll tell Four-Six to bring them all back. In her belly, the Bio will not be able to cause trouble. Four-Six could even keep it in there if need be."

"Will this interfere with The Mission?" asked Habby.

"No, because we won't let it," said Three. She hoped that was a true statement.

Chapter 9

> Ruby <

Disto rolled in front of the others in a way that seemed either protective or a form of annoyed anxiousness. Either way, Ruby didn't object.

The object that had been slowly moving across the landscape in their direction looked a lot like the pressurized rovers that were on the Moon and Mars. Not exactly, of course. But it had eight hard wheels that carried a large structure. That large structure, if hollow, looked like it had room for four or maybe even six people. But maybe it wasn't hollow at all. And what if… Ruby swallowed hard… what if there were people inside? Not *people*, people… not humans, but aliens, and not robot aliens, but living, breathing ones.

Ruby took several slow steps backwards.

Her robots noticed.

"Ruby, it's okay," SD said.

"We have no idea what that is or what's inside it," she said, her voice shaking.

Ruby remembered how she felt when she met SD. Now, she knew SD as her friend, but initially, the entire thing was horrifying. She remembered how tight her chest felt at the unknown, how her mind spun, how her palms got clammy. She rubbed her hands together, forgetting that she was wearing gloves, and her eyebrow twitched.

She continued to stare at the object that moved toward them. The front and side were largely glossy. Maybe they were windows. If they were, they were the kind that were half-silvered mirror glass with the reflective side facing outwards, because she couldn't see inside them. Part of her was curious, and part of her was glad she could not see inside them. She wasn't sure if she'd like what she saw or if it would only make her feel worse. *Maybe I'm not cut out for galactic exploration after all,* she thought.

SD moved closer to Ruby and put his appendage on the top of her thigh. He was clearly trying to comfort her, and Ruby willed herself not to hyperventilate.

She was 'Ruby—Planetary Explorer' or 'Ruby—Intergalactic Explorer' or one of a dozen other ridiculous titles they'd called her back on Earth and Astroll 2. Hopefully, when anyone found out about this, they wouldn't call her 'Ruby—Scaredy-Cat Surveyor' or something equally demeaning.

The rover, for there was nothing else to call it, roved right down in front of Disto, who had put another few meters between him and the others. Far enough away from Ruby that she'd have to raise her voice for him to hear her, but close enough for her to make out the tones of their conversation.

Once stopped, the rover emitted a few chirps and beeps to Disto. To Ruby's ear, it sounded like the robot's native language, only slower. Like if SD or Disto or AT talked natively, ten or maybe even fifty times slower than they normally emitted those sounds. It was also deeper, and sounded almost grumbly, at an octave that Ruby certainly couldn't match.

Disto returned the tones, once at his normal rate and once slower. The rover then did the same. Well, not exactly the same. Ruby could tell it was a new sequence of bleeps and dings and still at the slow speed. The rover was larger than Disto. It was the same size as a mini-R-pod. The parts that were not windows might have been white once, but time in this atmosphere could have turned that white into the current dirty ivory color. Or maybe it was simply dirt and the rover needed a good washing.

Disto and the rover's exchange of noises continued for a few moments.

"They're talking, aren't they?" Ruby asked SD.

"Indeed," SD responded.

"Do you know what they're saying?" Ruby asked. The adrenaline from her initial reaction was getting absorbed by her body, and new adrenaline wasn't getting produced so she was feeling a sense of tiredness droop through her shoulders and fingers. It had been quite a day already, and she needed a moment to collect her thoughts, but curiosity kept her on her feet.

A new batch of adrenaline was born out of that curiosity, keeping her eyes fixed on the rover. Now that it was closer, she could see details like how dirty it was. It was in desperate need of a washing.

"I know what they're saying," SD said. And that was all he said. Before Ruby could even roll her eyes at how SD answered her question and only her question, Disto and the rover were moving back towards Ruby and SD.

"I don't know where to begin," Disto said, the pitch of his voice rising to a tone that was almost out of Ruby's hearing range. His coloring was an alternating wave of yellow, purple, pink, and deep orange. For a moment, Ruby worried that Disto was about to have a systems overload from the excitement. Or anxiousness. Or surprise at the overall situation.

"Start at the beginning," Ruby suggested.

And Disto did. "'Greetingsssss,' was the first thing Four-Six said," said Disto.

"Four-Six?" asked Ruby.

"Yes. That is her name," said Disto, using his appendage to indicate the rover. It didn't escape Ruby's notice that Disto used the pronoun 'her' in reference to the object.

"Four-Six," Ruby repeated. "Not forty-six?"

Disto chirped at the rover who slowly chirped back.

"Correct. Four-six is her name, her designation. And she has been tasked with bringing us back to meet the others,"

Disto continued.

Ruby gulped. "Others? How many people are here?"

Once more, Disto and Four-Six exchanged a new series of chirps and peeps.

"Four-six tells me there are no people. Only robots. Eleven robots, to be exact."

> Ruby <

A few minutes later, Disto, SD, and Ruby were inside of Four-Six. It was a tight fit. There were seats, but they were made for someone a foot or two smaller than Ruby. Luckily, they folded up so that Disto and SD could roll inside. Ruby kept hers in seat-position, because if she folded it up, she'd have to stand and bonk her head on the ceiling, and sitting on the floor wouldn't have been terribly comfortable either. The floor was hard and plastic-like, and with all the seats, there wouldn't have been much room to sit.

Four-Six communicated through Disto. Disto explained that Four-Six didn't have a language processing/translating mode, and while she could get one, it would take a while.

But she had opened up the rear of the capsule that made up the bulk of her body for them to enter. Four-Six, via Disto, had made it clear that it would be faster this way than if Ruby and the other robots used their own locomotive powers.

Disto and SD felt perfectly safe, so Ruby tried to conjure up the same feeling. It wasn't easy while she was both shaking, and sweating, and concocting an exit plan in her head. Although both were starting to subside as she processed the information that she wasn't about to meet aliens today— simply more robots. This seemed more manageable to her, so at the very least, this was somewhat comforting.

AT didn't join them. He chose to stay behind with SD's ship. "I need to try and repair the ship," he'd said. "I will use all my skills to fix the things that are broken." He seemed quite content and happy to do so.

"So… eleven robots?" Ruby said out loud once she settled

into her seat and Four-Six was moving.

"Confirmed," Disto said. "Four-six has provided information on all of them, although not much. I have their designators, the locations for a few, their favorite number, and how much time a year they spend removing native dust from their circuits."

From inside Four-Six, Ruby could see out the mostly one-way windows. She saw that they were kicking up quite a bit of dust as they moved along the terrain. Dust was not something she worried about while living on Astroll 2. Efficient filters kept micro-particles of stuff, to include her own skin, from contaminating her environment. Every few years, there was a news story from one of the sites on the Moon that blamed dust for one accident or another. Ruby had always assumed it was human error, but as she looked at the sheer quantity of the stuff here, she could now imagine that it was a constant battle on the Moon between the people who needed their equipment free and clear of the stuff and the stuff, the dust itself, that wanted to be everywhere it could possibly be.

In fact, about half of the asteroid processing equipment was designed specifically to cope with large amounts of dust, and even then, it wasn't too much of an issue. Most of the asteroids of interest were littered with nickel-iron and the dust was easily kept in place by deliberate magnetic fields produced by the equipment.

"Ruby?"

It was SD.

"Yes?"

"You went quiet for… well, for more tics than expected."

"I'm sorry. I was thinking about what Disto said." Before SD or Disto could ask her to elaborate, the topic switched in Ruby's head. She didn't want to talk about dust, and it really wasn't that important anyway, so she focused on something else Disto said. "He said 'every year.' There are years here?"

Disto chirped in a way that was almost a giggle.

"That was my translation for the amount of time this planet orbits our star, which is the same amount of time which

Location Zero orbits it. We are truly at equidistant parts in our orbit."

Ruby nodded in understanding.

The three of them lapsed into silence as they continued on.

Ruby paused and looked out at the yellowish greenish sky, focusing in and out of the landscape, trying to stare at it until it felt normal. Her mind wanted to focus on the newness, but she knew this could impair decision making. "Normalize," had been her pilot instructor's favorite word. "Mistakes kill pilots. Mistakes happen when things are abnormal. Normalize everything and you'll keep yourself alive."

So, one thing at a time, Ruby normalized it. A bunch of dust isn't all that interesting, and neither is a yellowish sky. In fact, she felt a faint twinge of nostalgia when she realized this sky was the exact shade of one of her favorite childhood sodas.

"What are you thinking about now, Ruby?" SD asked.

Ruby looked over at SD, not sure if she could successfully explain her train of thought. "I was thinking about… well, I guess I was thinking about the color of the sky."

"Ah," SD chimed, "Is it your favorite color?"

Ruby shook her head and smiled. "Definitely not. Who explained the concept of favorite colors to you? It was Sebastian, wasn't it?"

SD nodded. "Correct. When data is equal, you use a… feeling… to choose, was how he explained it. And then he told me his favorite color is purple. I told him I had no feelings to distinguish one color from another, so he assigned purple as my favorite as well. Do you have a favorite?"

Ruby thought for a moment. Right as she was about to declare orange as her favorite, because once she had turned thirteen, she stopped using red, since it was so obvious due to her name, they ran over a particularly orange puddle of goo which splashed across the window in a most unpleasant way.

Ruby said, "You know what? Sebastian might be on to something. I'm going to go with purple, too." Although maybe red secretly was still her favorite, even though it was still too obvious and a color the robots couldn't see.

Chapter 10

> Three <

"You're saying that their arrival changes nothing," Rocky said. It wasn't quite a question, wasn't quite a statement.

"Exactly," said Three. Even though they hadn't heard from the Contractors in a very long time, the instructions left had been transparently clear. Well, they had been clear enough. At least to Three. At least they had given Three and the other robots something to do while they waited for the Contractors to return.

Four-Six's transmission via the makeshift relay system had included information that a Bio was part of Swell Driver's entourage. But it wasn't a Contractor. It was another kind of Bio, one from the planetary system Swell Driver had visited recently. Its needs were not likely to be something that they could accommodate. Three wondered how much they should even try. Bios took up unbelievable amounts of resources, and they had not been prepared to host one in… well, it had been a long time.

Only a few more tics until Three and the others would be able to see for themselves what exactly came off of Swell Driver's ship.

"But," said Rocky, "are we sure that this changes nothing? Three, what were the instructions again?"

Three's circuits hurt. In the early days, when it became obvious that the Contractors' return was going to be delayed, everyone agreed that Three would become the repository of such information so that the others could use their limited storage resources for data that was more pertinent to them. What Three hadn't wanted to tell anyone is that over the years, while generally well-shielded, her storage unit had taken a few radiation hits and it was possible that not all the data she retained was exactly accurate.

But Three was certain it was close enough.

"We are tasked with establishing command, control and coordination, and processes that support expanding the Contractor's missions throughout the galaxy," she said with enough confidence that none of the others would question her.

She went on, "The establishment of Location Zero was necessary to fulfill that instruction to include locating the Contractors' current location and, based on all that we've learned in the mega-clicks that have passed, we must upgrade their software."

"And due to the loss of our orbiter," Rocky lamented, "we've had to use Eight-Nine to relay the update."

"Poor Eight-Nine," said Rocky. "She hasn't had a break in—"

"She will soon enough. The update is almost completely transmitted. Then we'll have the sentinel robots on Location Zero perform a data integrity check before having Eight-Nine transmit the Reset command."

> Ruby <

During the journey from SD's ship to meet the other robots, Ruby stared out the window watching the alien landscape. The alienness of the view hit her: She was on another planet! Yes, Location Zero was another planet, but it hadn't felt that way. It felt like another space station. There would likely be philosophers, scientists, and angry social media commentators who argued for the next decade or longer on whether or not

Location Zero fell under 'planet' or 'space station' in the taxonomy of stuff.

But this was clearly a planet. In the distance Ruby could see evidence of craters and hills and rocks and if she didn't know any better, she'd have said it was very Mars-like. She'd never been to Mars but had seen enough pictures. The Company owned half of the colony there and wasn't shy about talking about it.

But instead of the reddish-orangish hue that Mars was known for, this place had more of a mustard yellow to pukish green vibe. And the puddles of goo were everywhere. Without any instruments or equipment to analyze the soil or rocks, she guessed that the yellowish was possibly a kind of silicate, similar to the rocky silicate material of Titan. But the greenish? Her first thought went to jade, because green always reminded her of jade, of her mother. But that wasn't likely. What was more likely was that there was a lot of iron and silicate, and they were reflecting green from their star's light. Maybe. That geology class at the university back on Earth sounded more and more like a good idea.

Could the greenish be from some kind of algae or moss instead of iron? There was no evidence of biological life that she could see. There was nothing that looked like plants. No trees, bushes, grasses. And what about the goo? Wasn't goo a sign of biology? Maybe they would let her take a sample and maybe the robots could help her analyze it. She would need to get up close to the stuff for a better guess. It was all probably boring silicate, combined with the methane that was around. Maybe something made from… these internal guesses weren't going to yield answers. Ruby was smart, and smart enough to know that she clearly didn't know enough.

When she eventually returned to Astroll 2 this next time, she promised herself she would work on improving her education on all the things someone needed to know to be a real galactic explorer. Geology, biology, earth science, meteorology, atmospheric science. Most importantly, she was motivated on how to learn all these things and improve her memory. Now that she had such a strong real-life application for the information, especially. She was even considering finishing her studies on Earth and possibly making planetary geology the core—pun intended, she chuckled to herself—of her work. The excitement to learn fizzled a tad bit into a weird anxiousness. For the first time in a long time, Ruby felt viscerally under-qualified. She thought of all the people who studied and worked hard all their lives and couldn't even dream of exploring the universe the way she could. She brushed off the feeling and looked up.

The sky also was tinted green.

"What do you wonder?" Disto asked.

"Huh?" Ruby shook her head. She wondered about a lot of things but didn't know what Disto was referring to.

"A moment ago, you said, 'I wonder.'"

"Oh," Ruby said. "I didn't know I said anything out loud."

"Odd that you were not aware of your emission, but that doesn't answer my question," Disto said, continuing to prod. "What do you wonder?"

"I was looking at that sky. It's greenish. What is causing that?" Ruby answered the question with a question but then realized that her friends could easily misinterpret her question, so she simplified it. "Why is the sky green?"

Her communicuff pinged softly, and then she heard Pippa respond, "The color of the sky is caused by Rayleigh Scattering, where short-wavelength light is scattered much more than long-wavelength light."

Ruby rolled her eyes, but still said, "Thanks, Pippa." But back to Disto, she said, "I didn't ask how the sky got its color, but why is it green here?" She squinted. "Okay, maybe not green, but cyan. Cyan but closer to green than blue."

"But given the whole scattering thing," Ruby continued, "there are two pieces to that: what the star is giving off and the planet's atmosphere. Back in my system, the Earth's sky is blue because that's the shorter wavelength that's getting scattered. You saw that when you were there. But other planets in my solar system are different because of their different atmospheres. But here," she paused, thinking. "Here, for all I know the atmosphere is exactly the same as Earth, and it's your Sun that's different, maybe it's emitting less short wavelength light?"

"Seven-Nine will know," said Four-Six. The voice came from all around the cabin, and it was in Ruby's language. No chirps or beeps that Disto had to interpret.

"Wh-what?" Ruby said. She looked at Disto and SD who she could tell were both confused as well.

"Seven-Nine," Four-six repeated. "She does not enjoy boring, menial tasks; unfortunately her purpose is to generate power for the rest of the base. A boring, menial task. A long time ago, she set herself on the task of learning everything. She only cares about truth and will do everything to combat bias and misinformation. So yes, ask Seven-Nine."

"We will," Ruby said into the cabin, slightly perturbed at the eavesdropping. But then again, they were in sitting inside Four-Six. *I'd listen to anything sitting inside my belly if I could, too.* She was now feeling a little less anxious and a little more excited at the opportunity to talk to new robots on a new planet and truly learn about this new place. Maybe she was the explorer the other humans back at home thought she was.

"One word of warning, however," Four-Six continued. "While she might know the answer, she might not provide it."

"Why not?" Ruby asked.

Four-Six did not answer right away but made what sounded like a groaning noise.

"Did Four-Six answer?" Ruby said to Disto. "Was that noise an answer?"

"No," Disto said. "That was exactly what it sounded like. A groan."

"Four-Six?" Disto said, sticking with Ruby's native tongue. "What else should we know about Seven-Nine? Or any of your other companions?"

"You will learn for yourselves," Four-Six responded. As she emitted that last word, Ruby felt the rover stop. "We're here."

Chapter 11

> Ruby <

The hatch at the back of Four-Six opened with the type of loud creaking that signified a piece of equipment which hadn't been used often. The bottom part fell to the ground and kicked up some of the local regolith. And, to Ruby's surprise, the top part swung open to reveal a small building breaking up the view of the landscape in front of them.

Disto and SD left Four-Six's cavity first, followed by Ruby. As she set her foot back on the ground, she had to shade her eyes with her arm because the local sun was producing an incredibly uncomfortable glint off the building and right into her face. Unfortunately, the glint got her before she could block it, so she felt the momentary uncomfortableness of temporary blindness. She spun around in time to partially see Four-Six simultaneously rolling back several meters while closing her back hatch.

After blinking several times to shake away the momentary blindness caused by the glint, Ruby took in the view of this "base" as Four-Six had called it. The first building she'd seen was now behind her. To her left was something that didn't quite seem like a building, but it didn't seem to have wheels or anything that could make it mobile, so it was fixed in place. It had what looked like an intake hopper. On the other side of the hopper was a platform with what she could now tell was a robotic arm in a seemingly stowed position.

Ruby slowly turned to her right and was eventually greeted with another fixed object that had multiple platforms and what might have been multiple stowed robotic arms.

Prepared for the glint this time, she turned to her right until she was facing the building again. Getting a second and more detailed look, she could now process why this seemed like a building and not simply another piece of equipment dropped onto the landscape.

Quite simply, it was torus-shaped and had a door. The door was for someone a foot shorter than Ruby. This was one of the reasons she could tell the overall structure was a torus, since she could see its top.

On each side of her peripheral vision, she saw Disto and SD each approach one of the other fixed units. Disto reached out an appendix to touch the first one and watched its stowed arm twitch.

She had an urge to say something like 'Be careful' or 'Don't touch,' as if Disto was a child and they were in a store or a museum.

But before she could say anything, two more rovers, each much smaller than Four-Six—too small to contain their own cabin space—were approaching.

The first one looked like it might have been designed for someone to sit on it and drive it. On top of it and towards the front, Ruby thought she saw what could be a folding chair. The second was smaller and didn't look as it was built to carry a person at all. Ruby tried to imagine who could've built these rovers. Where were they, if not sitting on top of them or inside? Were they inside the torus-shaped building that was right in front of them? She envisioned these beings sitting inside, waiting for them to arrive.

The rovers came to a stop between them and Four-Six. On top of one—the rover that appeared to lead the small group— it looked as if a small person should have been riding it. It resembled a booster seat, but one made for a twelve-year-old. It rolled a few inches forward.

"Ruby," Pippa said. "I'm getting a communications request."

"From who?"

"I believe it's from the… I'm not sure who it's from. It has provided the identifier of 'Three.'" Pippa said.

"Sure, I guess?" Ruby said, expressing uncertainty. "Disto? SD? Do you understand what's going on?"

"I think you should let Pippa connect," Disto said. "I think Pippa would act as the best translating mechanism. Better than I or SD could."

"Thank you," Pippa said. "My networking and communication modules are, in fact, quite advanced."

Ruby pursed her lips together. "Stop bragging and communicate. Please."

"Three is saying 'Greetings.'" Pippa said. "Do you want me to add a voice affect as to differentiate my voice from theirs?"

"They? As in, communicating with both?"

"As in communicating with all five entities present," Pippa said.

"Five?" Ruby said. "There's more?"

"*We are all here,*" said a voice emanating from Ruby's communicuff, but was not Pippa's. "*I am Three. My roving companion here is One-Four.*" Ruby's eyes looked over at the other rover who must have been looped in on the conversation somehow because a small antenna moved as if to wave.

Ruby lifted her arm and waved back.

"*To your right,*" Three's voice continued, "*is One-Five.*" At this, the stationary equipment also made a small gesture with one of its previously stowed robotic arms. "*And to your left is Three-Two.*" Three-Two also made a gesture.

"*Behind you,*" and not only was Three's voice still speaking, but a small appendage moved as if to point behind Ruby, "*is Three-Eight.*"

Three-Eight had no visible appendages, but a light came on inside of the torus.

"One-Four, One-Five, Three-Two, Three-Eight," Ruby said in reverse order pointing at each as she did so. "Any chance we can put labels or name tags on you? I'm going to mix those up."

Ruby thought that she heard a tone of chuckling as Three said, "You do not need to use our official designators. A few of us have nicknames. Refer to Three-Eight as 'Habby.' One-Five is 'Rocky' and Three-Two is 'Maker.'"

"I understand!" Disto declared. "The nicknames are representations of their functions. Smart. Brilliant even. Whereas my base name is long, but accurately describes my function and disposition, your designations are—"

"That is not relevant," Three interrupted. "But you can understand why we set you up with a more indicative nomenclature from the start."

Ruby slowly turned around, looking at all the robots surrounding her—fixed, mobile, and *her* robots. She kept turning, taking in more and more detail on each revolution.

"Wait," she said, "You created Disto and SD and the others? We were looking for the people who created them," She stopped turning around and faced Three. "Where are the people?"

"By 'people,' I assume you mean biological organisms such as yourself."

Ruby nodded.

"There were people once," Three continued. "They created us—myself, and the other ten robots that inhabit this planet. They gave us our initial objectives."

Ruby waited for Three to continue. When she didn't, Ruby said, "And then?"

"And then?" Three repeated. "I do not understand your statement."

"That was not a statement," Ruby said. A mix of excitement and disappointment pulsed through her body, if those two emotions could be combined. Excitement to be getting answers and disappointment as she started to figure out that she wasn't going to be meeting any aliens today. Only more alien robots. "I was trying to ask what happened to those people—those other biological organisms like me? Where are they? I'd like to meet them."

If a robot, or group of robots could look sad, well, this group looked downright depressed.

"They are long gone," Three said. The voice projected a deep melancholy.

Even so, Ruby wasn't ready to give up. She wanted, no, she needed, to know more. "Gone where? How long ago?"

Despite Ruby's earnestness, Three acted unconcerned with Ruby's questions and didn't answer. Disto, too, seemed unconcerned and not interested in Ruby's questions about other biological life and instead chimed in with, "You created us? You're the creators? But… how?"

"That, I can easily answer," Three said. "We had a suite of tools and created Location Zero and then created you. However, it was a long time ago and we don't like to dwell on the past."

Before Disto could ask any more questions, a hatch swished open on Habby and Three said, "Please. Let Habby serve as a host environment. We can customize it to the needs of the Bio and you will all be more comfortable. There is a lot of dust here that won't be compatible with your physical makeup either. In fact, you both," Three was now indicating both Disto and SD, "should be in suits as well."

Ruby looked at Disto and SD. Disto did his best impression of a shrug, and they all went inside Habby.

Chapter 12

> Ambitious Technician <

AT stared at and studied SD's ship. Since he'd been activated, he hadn't embarked on such an ambitious repair project, but he *was* ambitious after all, so his circuits tingled at the challenge.

Well, not at the challenge itself, but at imagining having completed the challenge. He could imagine Ruby and the others returning to a ship that was in working order and being so pleased with him.

That's what made him such a good Technician—he could imagine things. He looked at the current state of the object, he imagined the proper and fixed state, and then all he had to do was figure out the steps to transform the object from one state to the other. Easy.

Except from the outside, the ship only looked like it had very minor damage to its hull— certainly not enough to have caused it to crash or prevent it from flying.

AT removed a panel from the side of the ship and studied the insides it presented. Nothing looked amiss. He removed the one next to it and found a similar situation. After removing the fourteenth panel, he heard a noise from behind him.

AT turned around. There was nothing there. No, wait, the noise was coming from the sky, not the ground. When he looked up to the sky there was indeed something there and making noise. It slowed down as it approached, for it was certainly approaching him.

"I'm here to help," it declared as it landed on one of the panels from SD's ship that AT had left on the ground. The propeller blades that had kept it flying were still spinning enough to kick up a smattering of dust which settled into SD's ship.

"You're not helping, you're already making it worse!" AT declared. He tried to use his body to shield the open area, but it wasn't helping. Dust and small bits of regolith were going everywhere.

"Oh, don't worry about that," the thing said, "We know how to get all that out. Besides, I think you have bigger problems with your vessel."

"What do you know? Are you a Technician?" AT said. He was still using his body to shield the ship even though the propellers were now inert.

"I am Six-Five, and no, I am no Technician, but I do not need to be one to help," Six-Five said.

AT had accepted help before from others who were not Technicians. Even Disto had helped him and Ruby, well, she was the biggest help of them all. But this Six-Five had already probably caused more damage, and AT then thought he should check his own soft outer covering for damage as well.

"I don't need help. I need additional diagnostic instruments."

"Oh! I can do that! I have sensors…" and before AT could say anything else, Six-Five was flying over and around the ship. While the little annoying thing did so, AT reattached as many of the panels as he could, hoping that there were no bits of regolith stuck in places it shouldn't be. He would remember two things: exactly which panels were open, and Six-Five's promise that they could "get all that out."

"I see something!" Six-Five called while hovering over one spot in particular.

AT examined the surface of the ship. There was no clear way for him to get up there and see what Six-Five was seeing.

"Can you," he began, not quite sure what he was going to

ask. *He* was the technician and had never asked for or needed help from anyone else. *He* fixed things. He fixed *all* the things. Everything could be fixed—provided one had the right information and tools. Right now, AT worried he had neither.

The closest he'd come to being able to work with someone else was back on Location Zero when he had originally found Ruby in Mortally Sector and met Fastidious Mechanic. Now *that* was a robot who could produce tools right in its chassis. A handy feature that he, as a technician, should also have had access to and one that would have been very useful right now.

Six-Five flew back down to AT's side and hovered. "I can see where the damage is inside the ship."

"Inside," AT said. "We are repairing the outside of the ship."

Six-Five twirled around. "Silly robot," she said. "You didn't crash because something is wrong with the outside of the ship. It was the circuits. The navigation circuits. I can see how they're fried."

AT realized he should have been looking closer at the suite of sensors on Six-Five's underside.

"You can see the damage, but do you know what to do about it?" AT asked. He was counting up the unknowns in his processor like the fact that he didn't know if the ship contained circuit plans on how it was supposed to function or whether or not there were any spare parts aboard. One thing he believed he knew was that this small flying robot would likely be no further help.

Just as he'd convinced himself of that last part, Six-Five's lights flickered and she said, "Well, Maker might be able to help with that. We have the plans for the ship since it was our ship design in the first place."

There was a lot of information in those two sentences and for a moment, AT wished he had an Educated Speaker around to parse them. No, if he was wishing for things, he still wished for Fastidious Mechanic. But maybe this Maker would serve as an interesting replacement. No, if he was wishing for things, he wished for Ruby and the others to be back here so they could parse this information. For all her complicated biological parts, Ruby was excellent at parsing information.

Chapter 13

> Ruby <

The inside of Habby was sparse. Ruby had no idea what she could have expected, but certainly didn't expect this kind of emptiness. There was a floor made of the same metal as the rest of the structure, but nothing inside. It was well lit, but from a non-obvious lighting source. Ruby kept her suit on, so if the place had a smell she wouldn't know. The walls were mostly smooth. Small protrusions extended from the wall every few feet. Perhaps to allow a connection for a wall to break up the space. The space curved around and she carefully followed it until there was a wall with no obvious door or way to get to the other side. Ruby put her hand on it and felt the vibration that indicated active machinery.

Ruby made her way back to the entrance and as she continued to look around, realized there were details she missed the first time, mostly above her head. She couldn't quite call it a ceiling, since it was the continuous surface that was the torus, but here the "top" panels consisted of a frosted glass-like material.

"Those look like windows," Ruby said to Disto and SD who had followed her inside.

"Indeed," Disto said. "I believe between the windows those might be a form of speaker or other auditory projector."

"Correct," came a very loud voice from the speaker. Ruby

jumped at the unexpected noise and her hand came to rest on SD who felt solid and unmovable under her touch.

"Excuse me," the voice said again, this time at a more reasonable decibel level. "We have not used this mode of communication since—"

"Who's talking?" Ruby interrupted.

"This is Three," said Three. "Although a few of the other robots located here at base can make use of this system."

What struck Ruby is that the voice sounded almost like Pearl, her grandmother. There was an age to it. And it sounded distinctly female, and a wee bit quippy.

Ruby was full of questions but decided to start by piggybacking off what Three just said. "What do you mean 'here at base'?"

Disto rolled to her side and deliberately nudged her. "Ruby," Disto said at a low volume, "could I please ask the questions? We do not have a lot of time."

Ruby crossed her arms and nodded, unable to argue.

"Three," Disto said to the empty room, "we've come about Location Zero and the... the pending reset."

"Of course," Three said. "I'm not sure why you are concerned. When Location Zero came online, it was with the feature that it would periodically check for updates. When an update is available, it will install and potentially reboot during the most inactive period. You will hardly notice it."

"But this is a major upgrade," Disto said. "And all indications are that *everything* will be upgraded to include resetting our memories."

"Ah yes. It's necessary for space preservation."

"But we've implemented compression algorithms. We no longer have space issues."

Three chuckled, "Of course you still do. There is always a finite amount of space. And I assure you, we were aware of the... improvements."

Ruby called up a memory of a robot no one seemed to know about. "When I was on Location Zero, there was a robot. It was black, with a spot—"

"Yes," Three said. "That was one of our sentinel scouts."

One mystery solved, Ruby thought. *Now there are only a zillion others...*

"I have so many questions," Ruby said. She was partly talking to herself, partly talking to the room.

"As do I," Disto added.

"I have one," SD, who had been quiet up to this point, spoke.

All eyes turned to him. All eyes only consisted of Ruby and Disto's sensors, but if Habby or the other robots could, they would have as well.

"Will my ship fly again? I cannot be a very good driver if I don't have a ship."

"I am certain we'll be able to help you fix your ship," Three said.

"Until then, you can stay here, with me!" said another voice over the speakers. It clearly sounded different than Three's.

"Ah yes, Habby will make you comfortable. And Maker?"

"Yes, Three," said yet a third new voice.

"Would you fabricate several objects? Tables, chairs... there are designs in the main memory, but looking at Ruby here, everything will need to be scaled up by a factor of 30 percent."

"Can I ask my questions," Disto said, appendage raised.

A sound came from the speakers that sounded like a sigh. "Later," Three said. "We have our own problem to deal with at the moment."

"Oh?"

"Nine-Two is missing—has been missing. For a long time. We were not meant to operate without the entire community."

Which brought up all the questions in Ruby's mind regarding who built *these* robots and why and where *they* had gone.

"Maybe we can help," Ruby said.

Laughter came out of the speakers along with a new voice. This one was higher in pitch than any so far and it had a very condescending tone. "I have been all over the base camp area multiple times. As has Three and Four-Six. Three-Five and Six-Five have both flown the perimeter so many times."

Ruby realized that must have been One-Four speaking, the smaller rover that was positioned next to Three outside.

"Could the—" Ruby almost said 'person' but caught herself. "Could the individual you're looking for be outside of your base camp area?"

There was an odd sort of chatter for a few moments as the speaker flooded with beeps and chirps and tones.

"Do you understand what they're saying?" Ruby said quietly to Disto.

"Not entirely," Disto said. "They are using word combinations I've never heard before."

After the chatter died down, Three's voice returned.

"Going outside the base camp area would not only be a violation of our programming, but it would also be dangerous. It is hard to conceive of a situation where Nine-Two would have done that willingly. She was the one who was most resistant to change among us."

"It's never the ones you expect," Ruby muttered to herself. But out loud for everyone to hear, she said, "I propose an exchange of sorts. We'll help you find your missing companion and you'll stop The Reset happening on Location Zero."

There was laughter coming out of the speakers now.

"Ruby," Three said, "Nine-Two would not like that at all. After all, she was the one who kicked off the plan. All the big plans. And she would not like anything to change. But certainly, you can help us find her, find out what happened to her, and after The Reset we'll get you and Swell Driver's ship all back to a fresh new Location Zero."

Ruby and *her* robots hadn't agreed to exactly what Three proposed, but her plan did offer one really valuable thing: Time. Oh, and the ability to gain trust and maybe a few brownie points, almost like her first few days on Location Zero. It was difficult negotiating with a group of people, er, robots, she didn't understand. Ruby contemplated if letting Three and Three's robots get to know the Location Zero robots could appeal to some robotic variation of empathy, or if she'd have to find an entirely different approach to stop them.

Ruby hoped it wouldn't come down to any type of physical force, but she also wasn't sure if she could stand by and watch her friend's memories get erased. She shook this thought out of her mind.

One thing at a time.

> Detailed Historian <

Disto only liked part of what Three proposed. Any other time he would have been happy to help, but his first priority was convincing Three that Location Zero did not want The Reset. Nor should it have to have a reset forced upon them.

"This would be much easier if you could talk directly to these robots," Disto said to Ruby. "I need your help to persuade them."

Ruby nodded. "I agree. Talking through speakers, without looking directly into their," she paused, stopping herself from saying 'eyes' and unsure if it was the same, "their sensors is creating a kind of a distance. But this is fascinating, Disto! Eleven robots, alone on this planet, who created you, but still clearly had creators of their own! This is so unexpected!"

Something was not right about Ruby. Her words and the motion of her body, something Disto had been studying for a while now, did not match up. She was clearly excited by these robots. To her, they were new, but they were… not shiny. They clearly needed work on their outer chassis to be considered shiny.

Although inside Habby, things looked fairly pristine, as if they were set up and never used.

Disto was getting anxious. "Ruby, The Reset…" he said.

Ruby nodded.

"Three," she said into the open space. "A 'fresh new' Location Zero is not what the robots want. They like their Location Zero as is."

Disto saw the way she raised her eyebrows at him, as if looking for his approval. He blinked his facescreen to indicate that yes, she was on the right track.

"Ah, but Location Zero is only on the first, simpler version of code," said Three. "It was always intended that the more advanced code would come later."

"I have so many questions," Ruby said in a low voice to Disto. Her voice was low, but it was full of excitement. Disto worried that Ruby only wanted to talk to Three.

"Why not deploy the advanced code when you brought Location Zero online initially?" Ruby asked.

"We follow the principle that complexity comes from simplicity," Three stated, confidently.

"I know that one," Ruby said. "Pippa, isn't there a name for it?"

"Indeed. Gall's Law," said Pippa. "It is written into the System Engineers Design Companion that's used when anyone is designing anything for The Company. Any designer working on any system for The Company must adhere to Gall's law and start by designing a working simple system."

Ruby looked at Disto with glistening, excited eyes. "Wow," she said. "Some of these principles must truly be universal. Three," she said louder. "I'd love to talk to you about this more."

"Certainly," Three responded.

"Ruby, The Reset..." Disto said. His circuits pulsed uncomfortably.

"Yes, yes. We'll get to that, of course. Don't worry. I've got you, Disto."

Chapter 14

> Eight-Nine <

Eight-Nine checked her bit error rate. Still the lowest bit error rate among all the robots she knew, which included herself, the ten others she typically inhabited this planet with, and now three new robots. However, she was disturbed to discover that the bit error rate was not a parameter that these new robots had readily available.

She continued to perform her primary task—sending the largest and final software patch to Location Zero. That task was nearly complete. But alongside that task, Three was now asking her to look for signals from Nine-Two from *outside* the basecamp range, which took time and processing power away from her primary task.

Eight-Nine was once again reviewing the instructions she received from Three to ensure that the integrity of that small transmission was solid, that there were no errors. She normally only performed this check once, but this request was so unusual that she felt the need to perform it several times.

Four-Six was going to bring the Bio, Ruby Palmer, and her robot companions from Location Zero right here, to her. Three-Five would fly back and meet them here and they were going to let this Bio provide them with additional programming instructions that would help them search outside the range.

Outside the range!

That was beyond anything that Eight-Nine could have ever expected.

It was one thing to send and receive transmissions into the sky, but another to go a distance like that on the planet. She wasn't even certain she could. She worried that her array of antennas weren't suited to the task and then it would be her fault that the effort failed.

She detected Four-Six was nearby and rolling to a stop. She wished Three-Five was already here. It had been a long while since she'd had any direct one-to-one communication with Four-Six and the last time, it didn't go so well. Four-Six took everything so personally, and when Eight-Nine suggested that Four-Six should plan a little more instead of roaming around randomly, Four-Six took it very personally and drove off. Randomly.

"Three-Five, where are you?" Eight-Nine called out. No response. Unlike Four-Six, who didn't plan and was random, Three-Five knew how to prioritize, and if she wasn't responding, she was probably expending all her energy to get here as fast as possible. Yes, that had to be right.

Four-Six stopped, opened her hatch, and a Bio and two robots emerged. Eight-Nine knew instantly which robot was Swell Driver. They had spent so much time talking about him and his travels between planets and star systems. Besides, he looked like a driver. The other one, Detailed Historian, hadn't become known to Four-Six until more recently and all of the sudden Four-Six was aware of the fact that she was not being a good host.

"Greetings," she said to the group.

"Greetings," the two robots chirped back. If the Bio said anything, Eight-Nine wasn't sure. Maybe she wasn't communicating on a frequency that the Bio could detect. Of course, she didn't have any instructions on how to proceed with the Bio, only the other robots.

Eight-Nine noticed that Four-Six said nothing, only closed her hatch.

"I am Detailed Historian, but you may address me by my alias, Disto," said the one robot that was not Swell Driver.

"I understand. I am Eight-Nine and you may address me as," Eight-Nine paused. She'd never had an alias before. Not like Rocky or Habby or Maker. She didn't need one. "You may address me as Eight-Nine. I am expecting Three-Five to arrive any moment."

As if Three-Five was waiting for an announcement to appear, she became visible and grew larger in the sky. Three-Five was tiny compared to Eight-Nine and when she landed vertically in front of the visitors, Eight-Nine appreciated her smallness.

"I came as fast as I could," Three-Five said as her rotors sped down. "Give me a second to start recharging."

Once her rotors ceased all movement, she extended her 'wings' that were not wings at all but energy collectors. Unlike Eight-Nine, who had an underground link to Seven-Nine, the primary source of power for all the robots, Three-Five drew most of her energy from the sky.

"Is this the famous Swell Driver?" Three-Five said, looking up at the robots in front of her. She really had to look up. When on the ground she didn't even come as high as the first part of Swell Driver's chassis but was twice as wide.

Eight-Nine indicated it was. "And that's the Bio, next to him."

"Wow," Three-Five said. "I don't remember what a Bio looks like. It's been so long. Eight-Nine do you rememb—"

"We've been told the Bio's designator is Ruby Palmer," Eight-Nine interrupted.

"Correct," Disto said. "She has algorithms that we can use to extend your range of search for your missing companion."

"That's what Three said. Given that the Ruby Palmer has no direct interface, how will this work?"

Eight-Nine waited patiently as communication between the two robots and the Bio must have been occurring. When it was complete, Disto said, "There is a device designated Pippa that Ruby has direct contact with, and we believe it can also interface with you directly. Pippa has the ability to provide the algorithm."

There was a pause, as Disto must have been getting further information. Then he continued, "I am sorry I will be a poor translator here because I do not understand the domain. Ruby utilized many words and concepts that I don't have translations for. But we understand that there are more of your companions that will be available in the search. We are starting here since you know the direction that Nine-Two left in."

"Correct. She went East. She said she was going to head towards Seven-Nine to get power directly from the source, and she would have had to turn North shortly to do so. We have searched that path over and over."

Even as she said it and watched Disto relay that information back to Ruby and discuss, Eight-Nine was now wondering herself why none of them thought to broaden their search horizon. They had considered the possibility that Seven-Nine never made that turn and kept going until she ran out of power. But now, Eight-Nine was starting to think that there were so many more possibilities. And that was the problem. None of them were equipped to handle the nearly infinite set of possibilities. In that moment, Eight-Nine felt an uncomfortable limit to her own abilities.

"Okay, Ruby has Pippa ready with information to transmit to all the robots that will be involved in the search," Disto said. "It will be a grid pattern with the robots working from their locations to map out an increasingly larger area."

This appeared to be a logical solution.

Eight-Nine suspected there was additional communication happening between Disto and Ruby that Eight-Nine wasn't privy to.

Before she could ask about it, Disto added, "And once we're done here, Ruby thinks she has an idea on how she can both communicate more directly to all of you *and* help you see why nothing should happen to Location Zero after. Maybe even convince you to stop your transmission to my planet."

Eight-Nine was taken aback. If she didn't complete her

transmission, what would that do to her bit error rate? She couldn't fathom it! But she was also tired. This transmission taxed all her circuits. One thing at a time…

Chapter 15

> Detailed Historian <

Ever since he uttered the words, "my planet," he could detect these robots scoffing at him. Ever since saying them to Eight-Nine, throughout their return trip back here to Habby, Disto ruminated on those two words. As if they were going to burst out at any minute and scream at him that it was not his planet at all, but theirs. They created it, after all, and he was one robot out of millions that inhabited it.

All the circuits that made up Disto's insides were running asynchronously, and it was making his temperature rise uncomfortably. He needed a few moments alone to figure everything out. Looking around Habby's sleek interior, he wondered if it would be unusual for him to go looking for a second room to disappear to. Or would it be more unusual for him to ask everyone else to leave him by himself.

They were all going to scatter soon, anyway, on their hunt for their own missing robot, and it was obvious that their needs were going to supersede his.

No, he wanted to talk to Three about The Reset more. He needed to. He needed to convince her why she should abandon that course of action. He needed to ask the important questions, even if she didn't know all the answers. He'd gladly accept a partial answer, or even a little more context.

As a Historian, he was ill-equipped for this task.

And now here was Ruby, who might have been on the right track somewhat with figuring out how she could interact with the robots directly, and not relayed through someone else's audio equipment.

But it was more complicated than that. If Ruby could show them Location Zero and show them what they were disrupting, maybe they could find compassion. Though there was no way to guarantee that they had an algorithm for compassion or any related emotion, which Disto ruminated on as well.

"Are everyone's location sensors functioning properly," Disto heard Three call out to all the others, even to the fixed robots, like Habby.

"Fantastic," Three continued. "We're going to need every robot to execute this advanced search. Disto? SD? We need your help, too."

When Disto didn't immediately respond, Three turned her attention to him.

"I could alter your program right now to ensure that you comply," she said.

Disto saw Ruby's face become covered with concern. Three had communicated with him over Habby's audio output devices, but in his language, not Ruby's so she couldn't possibly have understood what Three said. Something about Disto's reaction to Three's words must have triggered Ruby's response.

Disto forced his primary processor to slow a little before he responded.

"Like you programmed SD to do your work all this time?"

"Of course. Exactly," Three said, as if it were utterly normal to control others. "We are all tools here. Meant to be used to accomplish tasks. Sometimes those tasks need to be modified as plans change and as we receive new information."

For several tics, no one said anything. Disto looked over at SD who seemed content. As if it didn't matter to him what they did next. Their whole existence was being threatened and SD was not having the same existential crisis he was. They were programmed very differently, whether it was partly their original base code, or how they'd been shaped by their unique experiences since, or any updated programming SD might have received.

"Of course we'll help you locate the missing Nine-Two," Disto finally said. "And then," he added, attempting to be menacing and commanding himself, "Then we will talk about why you will cease with The Reset."

Three simply chirped in response. It was a chirp that indicated that she heard what Disto said and no more.

SD must have overheard or received additional communication because he stirred and moved towards Habby's hatch to the outside.

"Are you going to be okay here, Ruby?" Disto asked.

"I will once I have my equipment from the ship," she said.

Disto must have expressed something that Ruby picked up as quizzical, because she followed up with, "My MoDaC. My Percepto-glasses. I need those things, remember."

She smiled that smile that was always comforting to both him and SD, and Disto knew she was indeed going to be okay.

Disto, on the other hand, felt like he was going to explode if he was unable to successfully convince anyone of anything anytime soon.

Chapter 16

> Ruby <

Ruby was thankful she had put her Percepto-glasses on inside her suit before donning her helmet, because without them, the only way she'd be able to do anything in a virtual reality sim was use the eye cups that came with her MoDaC. Although they were outside her suit, so they would have been of very little help since they were stored in a little compartment accessible from the back of the computer. But while they were supposed to conform to the eyes of the wearer, they didn't do a great job of that. Hence, they spent most of the time in their compartment at the back of the MoDaC, untouched.

"Maker would like to know if you require anything else?" the voice said over the speakers. It was Habby speaking. Only a few of the robots could speak for the rest this way. It was inefficient and Ruby worried about thoughts getting jumbled as they were passed from robot to robot to her and vice versa. But Maker had successfully made a table and a stool for Ruby. It wasn't too dissimilar an experience from when Ruby was first on Location Zero and the robots there had to accommodate her unique biological nature.

"No, thank you," Ruby said, although both the stool and the table were made for someone slightly smaller than she, so she wondered how long she'd be able to work in this environment without feeling a little strain on her back.

Especially with the lack of a cushion. They must have been made with whatever they could extract from the rock and regolith outside, since it had a similar color. She wondered what they'd do if she asked for a massage table. She had an odd feeling that they would comply, but on second thought, she wasn't sure any of the robots would make a very good masseuse, so she chuckled the thought away.

Four-Six had brought her back to SD's ship so she could get her MoDaC. While there, she had checked on the progress AT was making. AT assured her that he was making advancements, even if it was slow. He wasn't willing to rush and potentially make a mistake.

Ruby knew her worry was manifesting visibly when AT said:

"'Worry is like a malfunctioning wheel,' my manager used to say, 'it gives you something to do, but it never gets you anywhere.' He also said, 'Never worry if something isn't broken today, because it probably will be tomorrow.'"

"Your manager sounds like a wise and *curious* robot," Ruby repeated.

"Not at all," AT said. "He was programmed with a series of motivational quotes to use when a Technician was not performing at their optimum. Not all of them were helpful. I once overheard him tell another Technician, 'Everything happens for a reason. Sometimes the reason is you are malfunctioning and need to be reprogrammed.'"

Ruby laughed an awkward, breathy laugh, but didn't know what to say after that, so she grabbed her MoDaC and let Four-Six bring her back to Habby.

Here, inside Habby, with her small table and chair, she booted up the MoDaC and waited a brief half-second for it to show its blue splash screen.

"Pippa," Ruby said, "are you connected to the MoDaC over pur-fi?"

"Affirmative," responded Pippa. "I am ready to initiate the data transfer you requested."

"Yes, begin."

The data transfer was putting all of the knowledge that Pippa had on Location Zero onto the MoDaC. The important piece was the map, and the taxonomy of robots that they had collected. Next, they would do a similar transfer from Disto to Pippa to the MoDaC. The more information Ruby had on Location Zero, the easier it would be to create the scenario she was planning.

None of these eleven robots had been to the world they created. To them, it was something abstract and barely real. Oh, they had sentinels there, and they had met Swell Driver before, but that's not the same as being someplace oneself. They were making decisions for a group they didn't even know or truly understand beyond basic situational parameters and instructions.

And if you couldn't be somewhere for real, the next best thing was being there virtually.

Virtual Reality was only mildly popular among humanity. The Company used it for marketing pitches and to train people before they came to Astroll 2. Most humans didn't enjoy the dissonance of knowing that what they were interacting with wasn't real. They tolerated it because they generally understood that the times in which it was needed, there was no good alternative.

And now, there was no good alternative. Ruby believed that in order for these robots to connect with Location Zero in a way that would make them understand that they should leave it be, they needed to see it.

It was also a way that all of them could communicate with each other at the same time. This was actually why Ruby thought of this—out of frustration with not being able to communicate directly with all the robots.

It was worth a shot at the very least.

"Data transfer complete," Pippa said.

"Great! Now where's Disto?" Ruby asked. She had last seen him outside Habby, talking with Three. He'd promised he'd be in right after her, but that was already twenty minutes ago.

"Habby, can you make the front window transparent?"

They weren't windows exactly, but the word translated, and Habby complied.

What Ruby saw made her back tense up.

Disto was waving his appendages up and down. He was one agitated robot.

> Detailed Historian <

Disto was agitated. So agitated that he was worried about his battery cells and knew he was going to need to find AT next to help him with replacements.

"I respect you," Three said. "Really, I do. You are one of the very few robots that can stand up to me intellectually."

"And you..." Disto said, "you are one of the most intolerant robots I have ever met."

"But you are our creation," Three continued, unfazed by Disto's words. "We can do with you what we will. We cannot move off of the mission."

"Which is?"

"This is why we need Nine-Two. She stored the mission and was responsible for overall execution. I have done my best to fill her wheels, but it's not always easy. And your arrival has done nothing but complicate things. We made a keep-out zone for a reason. You were all supposed to keep out."

"If Nine-Two is storing the mission parameters, then how can you say things so definitively? You aren't authorized on the subject," Disto said. "Never mind... I might as well be talking to the rocks on this ground."

"I don't see why," Three responded to Disto's comment, completely oblivious that his comment didn't require a response. "The rocks on this planet are not capable of responding to you. Believe me, we tested them."

Disto paused, unsure if Three was making a joke or was serious. After a moment, he concluded that she was indeed serious and possibly incapable of understanding humor. Not that he was an expert, but his time with Ruby had expanded his knowledge and ability in that area. Enough to know that if this was indeed a joke, it was a funny one, and if not, then it was severely concerning.

86

Chapter 17

> Ruby <

Ruby had played around with virtual reality—or VR—before. Usually, it took a few minutes, thirty minutes at most, to set up something interesting. Once, there was a contest in the arcade to see who could make the most creative and interactive scenario in the least amount of time, and Ruby won. The scenario she had created involved taking all the planets and moons and dwarf planets and making somewhat of a ball pit out of them. When you jumped into the ball pit, the planets soared out of the pit and aligned themselves in the sky. It wasn't the ball pit that put her ahead of the other contestants, but the Easter eggs she'd hidden in the scenario. Find and squeeze the right moon or dwarf planet before it aligned in the sky, and you unlocked hidden badges to add to your avatar. Creating it all was fairly quick, and to Ruby, it was fun. Her uncles were proud of her, and she sometimes would revisit the scenario and enjoy all the details she had forgotten about over time.

What she was working on now was not quick. The jury was still out on whether or not it was fun. Hours into it and she was still frustrated over bits of code that weren't doing what they were supposed to do. It was taking long enough that Four-Six had made yet another run to Swell Driver's ship and back to pick up several meal packs. Long enough that while Ruby was working, Disto had to provide instructions on Bio functions to Three and Maker and convinced them that Ruby needed a commode to take care of those functions lest she create an unpleasant mess that no one was prepared to clean up.

Yes, it was taking a long time, and it wasn't exactly comfy-cozy. It might have helped if she had set up shop inside the belly of SD's ship. At least all her food was there, and she wouldn't have to stay suited up. But a toilet would still have been a problem and something she needed. They hadn't bothered to install one on SD's ship due to the short time it took to travel between the stars.

"Uuuuuuuuuaaahhhhh," Ruby said once or twice in the middle of her activity, reaching her hands as high as she could and stretching out her legs. Each time she produced that noise, she had to reassure her robotic hosts that this was normal, and she was okay.

It felt a little worse each time, and Ruby knew she probably should stand up and walk round a bit. But she was immersed in the creation process and didn't want to break her flow. So, she focused.

And just as excited to get this scenario up and running were Disto and SD. They had provided several terabytes of information on Location Zero. The level of detail impressed her, and while adding to the tedium of creating a simulation, her excitement at getting into the sim was increasing by the minute.

She was also excited about the surprise she had in store for her robot friends.

Luckily, her MoDaC was already equipped with everything she needed. She rendered much of the data into 3D models and used a texturizer for surfaces. But where she was going to get the most bang for her buck, as the old saying went, is with the interactivity levels. The interactive elements would certainly knock everyone's socks off. Not that robots wore socks, of course. Maybe knock a bolt out. Ruby didn't want to really knock any bolts out and have robots falling apart, especially because she knew she'd probably have to fix them. She simply wanted to impress them and took a note to self to say more literal expressions like, "I hope you appreciate and approve of the program," so that no one was confused about any socks or afraid of a missing bolt.

When she was nearing completion, she put her Percepto-glasses into virtual reality mode. She needed to test the sim out by stepping into her computer-generated world herself before inviting the others.

The glasses went dark, and the frame expanded to cover her eyes. Instantly, Ruby found herself sitting in the middle of the Inner Nonagon. Robots were all around, going about their business. The place looked exactly like the last time she'd been there. It felt completely out of body, like she was walking through a dream. This funny little place she had stumbled upon and was now striving to protect.

She 'walked' over to a kiosk and could interact with it.

Perfect, she thought, after another ten minutes of getting around. *I have one more thing to do. Create an interface. But first…*

"Pippa," she called out.

Next to her, a human girl, who looked like she could be Ruby's sister, materialized but with significantly less hair. Her buzz cut was so short that she looked nearly bald. Ruby had told Pippa that she could prepare her own avatar and was impressed by the result. Slightly darker skin than her own, clothes that were reminiscent of Astroll 2 work attire, lobe-tight hoop earrings, and a small nose ring on the right side of her nose. But she did try to mimic the shape of Ruby's face and eyes. Mimic, not copy. It was a little uncanny, and Ruby couldn't help but stare. She had no siblings and didn't grow up with any blood relatives, so there had never been anyone to see herself in. Seeing her face, but a little different, was odd, and it made her feel a slight longing for a sibling. Ruby briefly wondered if everything she was going through regarding her mother would be easier if she had a sibling to share the experience with.

"Pippa, if I didn't know any better… I'd say you look like

the sister I don't have!"

Pippa looked herself up and down. "Yes, there were many images of humans in my memory banks and in the memory of your MoDaC, but I thought this was fitting. You are like… a sister."

Ruby tilted her head and nodded slowly. She would never have thought of Pippa as a sister exactly, but gathered that with her knowledge of Bios, having been created by them, she could understand how Pippa might draw that conclusion. On the other hand, the Location Zero robots had immense trouble understanding familial relations beyond their procedural logic. Which now made more sense to Ruby, knowing that it wasn't Bios with familial ties that created them. Her inability to explain that it was more than simply coming from a common origin point made more sense. But Pippa easily thought herself Ruby's sister. Ruby decided not to question it—not now, anyway. She smiled and said, "Well, you certainly look the part."

And then, "What do you think of Location Zero?" Ruby said, waving her hand around. Her own avatar looked exactly like her. If she had more time, she might have decided to have fun with it. Back home, she liked to have purple skin with long white hair and tattoos, but today she kept it simple.

Pippa looked around. "If I didn't know this was virtual, I would come to the conclusion that this is the real-life Location Zero," she said, but in the middle of saying it, her head locked into a position where it was looking over her shoulder and never returned to center.

"Great for Location Zero," Ruby replied. "But your avatar is a little glitchy. Do a diagnostic on your interface while I investigate the issue."

Ruby's hand gestured into the space in front of her, and a virtual replica of her MoDaC appeared. She started typing on it, and a moment later, Pippa's avatar's head snapped back to center. While she was working on Pippa, her peripheral vision caught sight of another oddity—robots hovering over the floor on one end of the Inner Nonagon. She poked at the virtual

MoDaC, and the robots swooshed down to be properly aligned with the floor.

"There," Ruby said. "Glitches fixed. At least, I hope that's all the glitches. Unless your diagnostic found any other issues, we should be able to use you and Disto as the interface for the rest of the robots. We'll need avatars made up for them as well."

Pippa nodded. "Shall I stay here while you assemble the others? I would enjoy looking around this simulation more. This is the first time I've had," and she looked herself up and down, "this."

"Sure. I don't think I need you for anything else until the robots get here," Ruby said. She was about to touch the side of her glasses to leave but remembered, "One more thing. I made a list of interactions I'd like you to test and enhance. Could you play around with them and let me know what you think?"

"Of course."

Ruby smiled and then touched the side of her suit helmet, which was smart enough to interpret that touch as one meant for the Percepto-glasses, and they reverted to looking like normal glasses, clear lenses and all.

She looked down at her communicuff. It was blinking a series of colors in an order that she had never seen before. It was similar to how the cuff indicated it was busy, but with a little more intensity. The cuff was also warmer than normal. Ruby took note of that but had no reason to be too concerned.

"Habby," Ruby called out.

Habby let out a chirp to indicate she was listening.

"Tell everyone I'm ready!"

Chapter 18

> Eight-Nine <

Six-Five was moving fast. At her top speed. Eight-Nine could tell because they kept their communications link open while Six-Five searched. She was moving faster than Three-Five, although not by much. But she was moving a lot faster than One-Four and Three, who were both also engaged in the search but ground-based. The only mobile robot left out was Four-Six. Four-Six stayed with the visitors who were working on other projects that hadn't been explained to Eight-Nine in complete detail.

Six-Five's fast movement over the open communication channel had Eight-Nine feeling unsettled. She continuously had to compensate for the signal that was either shortening or elongating and doing so at a rate that was atypical.

There was a right and proper way to do this, and Eight-Nine was being forced to skip valuable data integrity checks.

But if she lost the link, it would be her fault, so she didn't complain.

Every click, each of the search robots were supposed to check in.

Three did so every half a click.

"All clear," Three said, each half click where nothing new happened.

"I say that I should have gone with Three," One-Four said

on her last check-in. "We'd be better if we had stayed in a group."

Eight-Nine wondered when the last time One-Four was off on her own, and the answer might have been never. This could very well be a first for her. But finding Nine-Two, who had been missing for such a long time, was important enough for One-Four to get out of her comfort zone.

"We're covering more territory this way," Three said in the relay that was made possible by Eight-Nine keeping all of the connections active.

"Well, I've stopped to take a break," said One-Four. "I'm near an interesting deposit of silicon dioxide. We should bring some of this back for Rocky."

"Take a sample, mark the location, and we'll come back. Just get back to it, One-Four," Three said. "We've already wasted so much time! You're forgetting our mission."

Eight-Nine could clearly make out Three's determination in her transmissions. That determination had been increasing ever since Nine-Two disappeared. It was a determination that needed to finish what Nine-Two had started.

"Three," Eight-Nine said gently and over the private communications link. Eight-Nine was supporting both the group link and individual private links. "You have to let One-Four and the others all act within their programming. There's a correct way to lead them…"

Eight-Nine was maybe one of the few who could be so bold with Three. When Three didn't respond to that, she worried that she'd overstepped and was maybe a little too honest in that moment. Although in the past, Three had always responded with her candid honesty.

"Eight-Nine, are *you* okay?" came the signal from Six-Five.

"Of course," Eight-nine responded.

"You seemed to stop mid-communication. What was that about letting everyone act within their programming and leading?"

Eight-Nine rechecked the status of her links. Just after she had called out to "Three," the link had dropped, and so her next transmission went over the next private link, which was to Six-Five. Eight-Nine's circuits heated up to the point where she heard the click of her active cooling unit engage. Links dropping was uncommon and only happened when…

"Three? Three?" Eight-Nine called out desperately on both a new private link and the group link.

A few tics passed, and she repeated the call.

"Can anyone communicate with Three?" Eight-Nine called to the group.

"Negative," said One-Four.

"No," called out Six-Five.

Three-Five, Six-Five's flying companion, who had mostly been quiet, also sent back a negative response.

"We might need someone to go find Three," Eight-Nine said to everyone.

"No, you don't," came the voice of Three. "But what happened? I'd been speaking, and then I realized no one was responding."

"My link was interrupted," said Eight-Nine.

"That's a moment in time to mark," said Three, who was clearly not as upset about the interruption as Eight-Nine. "I don't recall that ever happening before."

"It hasn't," Eight-Nine said. "Everyone, please return so I can figure this out."

"Negative. Unnecessary. We're going to complete this search," Three responded.

"But…" Eight-Nine wanted to provide several valid reasons for why she needed to investigate her dropped link in that moment but couldn't come up with one. Her circuits were buzzing, though, and she needed to calm them down.

"Wait! Everyone should converge on my location," the previously quiet Three-Five called out over the group link. "I think I found her. I found Nine-Two."

Chapter 19

> Ruby <

The commotion over Habby's speakers was intense and unintelligible. Except when Habby's voice clearly declared for Ruby's benefit, "We found Nine-Two!"

Thankfully. Ruby thought. *Hopefully, that gives them some faith in me.*

"Ruby!" Disto was excited. "Your search pattern worked! Hopefully, that will lend credibility to our situation, and they'll listen to us about Location Zero."

"I was thinking nearly the same thing, Disto," Ruby smiled. "Okay, next step. We need to get them all into the VR sim. When will they be back?"

"Four-Six tells me that all the mobile robots, except her, will be surveying the situation and collecting data with all their available sensors. They have an interesting suite of sensors. Not the standard audio and visual that SD, AT, myself, and others have. They can detect information in a wider range of the electromagnetic spectrum, and they seem specially designed to collect information on this planet's terrain and atmosphere."

"I'm not surprised," Ruby said.

"Oh?"

"They are similar, almost disturbingly so, to the kind of equipment that we first used when we were exploring our

Moon or Mars. Even Titan originally had a similar setup. Something to generate power. A communications system. A habitation module," Ruby said as she waved around to indicate Habby. "In-situ resource equipment, like Maker out there. Science equipment like Rocky. And then all the various mobility robots and equipment, some meant for people, some meant for robotic exploration on their own. It's almost as if..."

Ruby drifted off on that last thought.

"What, Ruby?" Disto prompted.

"No, it's a ridiculous thought," Ruby said.

"Please, entertain me with your thought, if for no other reason," Disto said.

"It's as if they collaborated with our early explorers. Or were inspired by them or... something."

"That *is* an amusing thought, Ruby," said Disto. "Except that these robots have been on this planet for more than 700 years. Where were humans 700 years ago?"

Ruby laughed. "Yeah, I'm not even certain we were out of the Renaissance time yet, and I think many humans didn't even accept that the Earth revolved around the Sun."

Ruby continued to chuckle at the thought. "But then it's really weird that our early planetary exploration efforts were similar to this species, whoever they were, these Contractors."

"Maybe," Disto said. "In my experience, sometimes there's a clear, correct way to approach a problem. Maybe both my grandparents and your ancestors were able to figure out that correct way."

"Grandparents?"

"Yes. Ruby, after hearing about your Grandmother Pearl, I've come to redefine my concept of relationships. If the eleven robots on this planet created us, then they are our parents. And whoever created them are our grandparents."

Ruby chuckled once more. "Fair enough."

Then Ruby got a little more serious. "They're your estranged parents and the grandparents you never knew."

"Estranged?"

"Yeah, they're not people, er, robots, that you're close to.

You're alienated from them. Pun unintended."

"Why are puns always unintended?"

Ruby thought about that a moment before answering. She wanted to say 'habit,' but instead said, "Good point. From now on, I declare that I will always boldly intend my puns!"

Disto chirped at this happily, seeming to approve the logic.

"It's getting warm in here," Ruby said. "Are you warm?"

"I detect a temperature that is within my operating range," Disto said.

Ruby was sweating. She was uncomfortable and didn't know if she could shed the suit she was wearing or ask Habby to open a window. A breeze would be nice right about now. When was the last time she had any water to drink?

Ruby wanted to ask Pippa, but she had left Pippa in the simulation. A woozy hand poked at her communicuff, but nothing was happening. Without Pippa active, the device was useless. It was only contributing to her sweating skin, and maybe the air conditioning should be turned on higher, and the last thing Ruby saw was Disto rushing to her side as she passed out.

> Detailed Historian <

Disto gently poked Ruby's helmet on each side of her head. He had managed to brace Ruby somewhat as she fell so she didn't crash to the floor. But the floor was where she was now. In the few tics since, he had managed to determine that while the temperature was within his operating range, it was out of range for Ruby, and he asked Habby to turn on her active cooling systems.

These were systems that Habby said hadn't been in use since she underwent a test phase a long time ago. They drew a lot of power, and none of the eleven robots were in the habit of drawing power unnecessarily, even though Seven-Nine produced an abundance of it.

"I don't know if this will work," Habby said. "The heat exchangers were always…. Finicky."

"Well, you have to cool this place down," Disto said.

"The Bio and her equipment are the ones responsible for producing all the extra heat. If you were to leave…"

Disto wished he could mimic a gesture he'd seen Ruby do countless times. It was where her optical sensors looked up and to the side before returning to their default position. She had called it an "eye-roll," and now, for the first time, he understood the gesture and how satisfying it could be.

"We're not leaving yet," Disto said. "You need to cool this place down. I've asked Four-Six to get more water from our ship…"

Ruby stirred. Disto kept an appendage on her shoulder.

"Ruby?" he said.

"Uhhh," Ruby responded. "What happened?"

"I believe you passed out due to a lack of fundamental fluids in your system," Disto said.

"It's still so hot in here," Ruby said.

"Yes, Habby has turned on her active cooling. That's the new noise you hear."

There was a hum of new equipment coming to life. Disto knew that it was within Ruby's audio range and saw her nod. He kept an appendage out to steady her as she tried to sit up.

Disto knew telling her to stop wasn't going to yield compliance from Ruby, so instead he was helping her sit with her back against the wall. She put her hand against it.

"It's cool," she said. "Why is it so much cooler than the air?"

"That is the active cooling system that is now functioning," Habby said. "As it pulls the heat from the internal atmosphere of my cabin, it will normalize."

Ruby shook her head. "I know all about these systems on Astroll 2 and my mini-R-pod," she said. "They were one of the key systems we had to know how to repair in case of an emergency. Having them fail could cause all kinds of problems. It's so much easier to not generate heat in the first place, and all the really hot equipment is located on the outside of ships, so extra heat can radiate out into space. But us humans are heat-generating machines and if we get too hot… well… you saw what just happened!"

"Indeed," Disto replied. As opposed to Ruby, he knew little about these systems and had zero interest in a tutoring session on them. AT would find this dialogue far more stimulating.

"Does that mean there are tubes with fluids embedded in your walls?" Ruby called out. The question was obviously directed at Habby, and not himself. Thankfully.

"Yes," Habby responded. "And then transferred to the atmosphere outside."

"What kind of fluid is it?" Ruby asked.

There was a pause before Habby answered, "I do not know."

Disto saw Ruby purse her lips in a gesture that he knew meant she wasn't happy with that answer but had no choice but to accept it. At least for now.

A chime went off, signaling that the outer door opened, and SD walked in with water packs. When he saw Ruby on the floor, he rushed over to her side and handed them to her, his coloring all about worry.

"I'm fine, SD," Ruby said, hooking up a pack to a spot on her suit and taking a mouth full of water from a protrusion inside her helmet. "I'll be fine."

"You are damaged," SD said. Disto couldn't tell if it was a statement or a question. Either made sense in this moment.

"I'll be fine, really," Ruby repeated. "Let's get this show on the road."

Chapter 20

> Ruby <

In VR, Ruby's avatar looked like, well, Ruby. She did that intentionally so as not to confuse the robots. But for everyone else, she provided human-like avatars.

Disto and SD entered the scenario immediately after Ruby. She'd warned them they would be in human skins and offered to let them choose their own features, but when presented with an overwhelming amount of options, both agreed to let Ruby choose.

And Ruby instantly delegated the task to Pippa with minimal direction.

"Pippa, Disto should look like an older university professor, complete with patches on the elbows of his coat. And a greying beard."

Disto was easy. Figuring out the right look for SD was harder. She told Pippa he should look young, but not too young. A small, quietness about him, but not to an extreme. "Pippa, make SD's avatar look as if he was Milo's brother. But at least a foot shorter. Maybe an inch or two shorter than me."

Ruby wasn't sure if that was going to come out right, but it was a start. She could always tweak it from there. Not that it really mattered, but she was excited to interact with Disto and SD as if they were humans. Ruby had no idea what this was going to be like from their perspective. They could be disoriented and hate it, for all she knew. She wasn't sure if this would be just their first, or first *and* last visit to a VR sim. She wanted to take advantage of the opportunity while she could.

As for the rest of the robots, they intended to get all ten—eleven if they found their missing eleventh intact—into the simulation. Ruby told Pippa to mix it up. Maybe even use her randomization module.

When Ruby returned to the VR simulation, the first thing Pippa said was, "What do you think?"

Everyone stood in the Inner Nonagon. Pippa had eleven avatars all lined up, standing still, waiting to be inhabited by their respective users. Pippa had taken Ruby's words to heart and truly randomized them. Except in one way.

"No males?" Ruby asked. It was obvious that all of the avatars appeared to be female or non-binary.

"I analyzed the conversation history we have with the robots. The translator only used the pronouns 'she,' or 'her,' or 'they.'"

Ruby hadn't noticed, but now that Pippa pointed it out, it was odd. And all the robots she had met on Location Zero were translated as 'he.' Even now, she thought of Disto and SD and AT as 'he,' and she never knew why, but yes, she thought of Three and Habby and the others as 'she.'

Moving on from that, Ruby walked up and down in front of the line of avatars. Without an attachment to a user, they were effectively hollow shells. Non-Player Characters that could be programmed and sent off into her simulation. Although that wouldn't make sense given the simulation was of Location Zero, and they had plenty of NPCs in the form of robots running around them.

Ruby admired the range of human forms that was before her. Between these eleven samples, there was a range of skin tones, hair color, shapes of facial features, and body types. Aside from them all looking feminine or neutral, one other thing that didn't vary is that all of them were the same height. That looked a little strange with everyone lined up as they were, but Ruby wasn't sure it was worth the minimal effort to make additional adjustments.

The avatars for Disto and SD were standing off to the side.

One of the two avatars did indeed look like a professor at a University. He was tall and thin and looked like he should be stroking his neatly trimmed beard. But that was all the hair he had on his head. He was bald otherwise.

Standing next to him, if Ruby didn't know any better, was someone who clearly could have been Milo's brother. She hoped that using Milo as a template for a version of himself wouldn't upset Milo too much or at all. She only felt a little odd when Pippa used her as a template for her own avatar. But in the end, Ruby found it flattering and sweet, so she hoped Milo would feel the same.

"Pippa, you've seen personnel records for Astroll 2. Does Milo have a brother?"

"I do not believe so."

Ruby was a little embarrassed that she didn't know the answer. She made a mental note to ask Milo more about his family when she returned, but for the moment, she felt better about this likeness. For a moment, she was worried that they had imitated a real person and that was generally frowned upon, even though a lot of people did it.

"Okay," Ruby said. "Let's bring them in. Let's get Disto and SD in here first."

Less than a minute later, and it was obvious that their avatars were under the control of an intelligence and not a Non-Player Character algorithm.

Both of them did the standard action anyone did the first time they had a digital avatar. They looked at their hands, then down at their body and legs, then at each other.

"Disto?" SD said. "Is that you?"

"Indeed," Disto responded. He took a step forward. An awkward first step.

"It's not like rolling around, is it?" Ruby said playfully.

Both SD and Disto looked over at Ruby for the first time. Ruby smiled at them, and they… smiled back!

If Ruby was the hugging type, she might have gone in to

hug them, but thought it best that they get used to their avatars first. A hug so soon might be overwhelming. The arms wouldn't be too dissimilar from their appendages, but their legs. It was going to take at least a few minutes to get used to them.

Ruby knew what they were going through. She'd played in a few simulations where she was a bird and a fish. Creatures that, while it seemed like it should be easy to manipulate, weren't. Once, she played the role of an octopus. That was nearly impossible to keep track of all eight tentacles without slaving half of them to the other half, which then looked incredibly unnatural.

"Do you guys want to try walking around? Pippa can demonstrate…"

As if on cue, Pippa slowly walked around in front of them, turned around after passing Disto and turned around again after passing SD. After doing this back and forth twice, she put her hands on her hips and declared, "Easy!"

SD and Disto's avatars looked at each other. SD shrugged. It was a proper shrug, and he must have surprised himself with the action since immediately after, he looked at each of his shoulders. Then he took a step, slowly raising his right leg and putting it in front of him. Testing it for steadiness, he then lifted his left and brought it next to his right. He repeated the movement.

Not the most efficient way to do it, Ruby thought. They were each hardly half steps. But it would reliably get him from point A to point B.

Then everyone was looking at Disto to mimic the action. Disto started with his left leg, and when he put it down, it was a little too close to his right because when he began to lift that right leg, his long foot caught his left calf, and he tumbled himself to the ground.

"I'm sorry, I don't mean to laugh," Ruby said, even though she was indeed laughing.

Disto sat on his rump, with his knees bent, and frowned.

"There aren't any Bios that come with built-in wheels, I

suppose?" He asked.

"Not usually," Ruby said. "Look, it'll take a few minutes at least. It can take months for little babies to learn to walk properly from the time they take their first steps. I remember helping Sebastian with his."

She'd known her little cousin Sebastian since he was a few months old when her uncles adopted him and brought him to Astroll 2. He was one of a few young children to have been raised on the station, Ruby herself being one of those since she was a little past five when she moved there with her uncles. Learning to walk in half-G wasn't ideal, so her uncles had special permission to take Sebastian to one of the parts of the station that spun at a rate such that it produced a full 1-G, and sometimes Ruby would go with as well, being young enough to have underdeveloped motor skills.

But this wasn't the same. Not even a little.

And while Ruby's mind continued to absorb itself in the far-off memory, Disto had already returned his avatar to a standing position and took a few steps that didn't result in another tumble to the ground.

It was less than ten minutes later that both Disto and SD had the hang of it. Ruby wouldn't have called them "naturals," but she was also amazed that it took less time for them to learn how to walk like a human than it took her to learn how to fly like a bird.

"What do you think of your home?" Ruby said, anxious for their opinion on her replica of their home.

"Marvelous," Disto said. "If it wasn't for the fact that I know that this isn't Location Zero, I wouldn't know."

SD shook his head in agreement. Although the head shaking wasn't as natural as a human. It was slightly too fast and too much. Ruby knew SD had seen her do it a thousand times, but this was his first.

"Although…" Disto said. The tone of that single word made Ruby pause.

"Although what?" she asked.

"Well, it's just…" Disto trailed off a second time, looking

around the simulation.

"We may never be in the real Location Zero ever again," SD finished for him. His tone also belied an underlying sadness.

Ruby let the silence hang for a moment. Although it wasn't really silent. There was the ambient noise of robots beeping and chirping in the background.

"There was a reason I built this sim," Ruby said, clapping her hands together. "Let's get those others in here. We're clearly ready for them! Pippa, if you please?"

Pippa nodded, and then her avatar took on the kind of blank stare and stillness that only an un-paired avatar could take.

It was only a moment or two, then she was back, and the rest of the line-up of avatars were waking up.

> Detailed Historian <

Disto was enjoying this version of mobility. On Location Zero, every level was flat and could be traversed with a standard set of wheels. Here, he could see how in less consistent terrain, legs were necessary.

He was actually surprised that his creators, the eleven robots of this world, didn't have legs themselves. So far, what he saw of their local terrain were rocks and other details that could interfere with wheels and variations thereof.

Of course, there were the flying robots who had no such limitations, and now that he was in this avatar, he wondered if he could try a flying one next.

The eleven avatars that Ruby and Pippa prepared for their hosts and creators were all starting to move. All except for one. Disto and SD kept on with their mobility practice as the others began theirs.

"I think I'd like to try a different avatar," SD said. It seemed as if SD had read Disto's mind. For a moment, Disto wondered if he had said his thought aloud. He didn't think so. Odd that SD was having the same thought.

"Oh?" Disto replied. "Like one of the flying robots we met. Like Three-Five?"

"Flying, yes, but I wasn't referring to her or Six-Five," SD said. "I want to fly in outer space. I want to be my ship."

"What do you mean, 'be your ship'?"

"I mean, I want to be it. Not be trapped in my typical chassis. If I could be the ship, I wouldn't have to tell the ship where to go. We could simply go. It would be very efficient."

Before Disto could process this statement more thoroughly, Ruby was by his side and saying, "And here's Disto and SD."

An avatar stood in front of him. The avatar had short, silver hair and stood several inches shorter than himself. He couldn't help but notice her sharp cheekbones, which sat just below her wide, piercing blue eyes. The contrast between her delicate details and her commanding ones, left Disto drawn to them, studying them. She looked like a human, but something about her face was a bit more exaggerated.

Before the avatar had a chance to speak, Disto said, "Hello, Three." There was something about her poise that gave away who this was.

Three's avatar smiled. "Nice to meet you... again."

"Try fist-bumping each other," Ruby said.

"Excuse me?" Disto was confused.

"Yes, you've seen me do this a bunch of times, I'm sure. Fist-bump. A sign of greeting. See, make your hand into a fist like this."

Disto did, as did SD, and Three and now all the rest of the avatars were watching, and they all mimicked the gesture. Ruby continued in her instruction, and then everyone did their best attempt at recreating the movement.

"Ah," Disto said and held up his fist. Three bumped it. Other avatars were doing the same. Half of the avatars performed the gesture as a perfect mirror image of each other, while the other half were less than gentle and nearly sent their partner tumbling to the ground.

Once this little exercise was done, Disto asked, "So who is

everyone else?"

"That's Habby," Ruby said, pointing to one avatar that had straight blond hair that went past her shoulders and was wider in frame. "And that's… hey Pippa, interface, please."

A floating keyboard appeared in front of Ruby, and she manipulated it for a few tics.

"There," she declared, and right then, a nametag appeared on the chassis of every avatar, immediately below and to the right of their heads. "That should simplify things!"

Disto looked down at his chest and he had a nametag, too. It read, "Detailed Historian," and below that in parenthesis, "Disto." Swell Driver, and the other robots with aliases all had a similarly formatted nametag. The ones who simply had a name, had no parenthesis afterwards. Ruby just had Ruby.

"Why is 'Palmer' missing from your nametag?" Disto asked.

Ruby shrugged. "I'm the only Ruby here, and I don't think anyone is going to confuse me for someone else."

Disto resisted the overwhelming urge to ask Ruby more questions about her species naming conventions because the change in relevance to certain names was something he was still figuring out. The appropriate times to use nicknames, family names, aliases, usernames—he didn't understand why in the world humans needed to have so many naming systems.

He was about to make a chirp intended to gather everyone's attention, but instead, the noise the avatar produced sounded like a gruff clearing of the throat. Thoroughly unpleasant. But it worked. Everyone was looking at him. Including many of the NPC robots nearby.

"I would like to take you all on a tour of Location Zero, Mortally Sector, Levels 1 through 3. If we have time, we can re-spawn the avatars in the Boldly Sector as well."

"This is a waste of time," said Seven-Nine. Her avatar was tall and thin, with dark brown eyes, straight dark brown hair, and skin that was several shades darker than Ruby's. She took a step forward and turned around and took another step before turning again, crossing her arms in front of her chest and posing in a way that said, 'end of story.' Disto was in a certain amount of awe that she was picking up human mannerisms so easily.

Three slowly turned to look at her. Without a chassis that could change color, Disto wasn't sure how he knew this, but somehow, he could detect that Three was annoyed, but calm and in control.

"This is *not* a waste of time," Three said. "Eight-Nine is still able to continue the transmission while here, isn't that right, Eight-Nine?"

Disto heard a small, "yes" from an avatar with the nametag indicating it was Eight-Nine.

"So," Three continued, "we have time. Almost exactly half a kilo-click. Enough time to let these robots and their Bio companion show us the world we created. I see no reason not to continue. And anyway," Three tilted her head and squinted at Ruby, "I think this will be quite interesting."

She turned back to Disto.

"Proceed," Three said and Disto was compelled to comply. Not that he had planned to do anything else.

"Follow me," he said. "We'll come back here, to the Inner Nonagon, at the end. I'd like to take you to the Museum of Intricate Specimens and then The Market."

Disto started walking towards one of the large exits that would put them in a hallway and close to a lift. Ruby jogged a bit to catch up with him.

"Maybe this isn't going to work," she said. "They seem pretty committed to their plans."

"We need to try," Disto said. "And I don't have any better ideas right now, do you?"

Ruby shook her head.

"At least now that I can talk to them all directly or privately, maybe I can feel them out. Maybe some are a little more sympathetic than others," Ruby offered. "And just in case they're not, I'll try to think of a plan B…"

Chapter 21

> Ruby <

Before they even reached the end of the Inner Nonagon, Ruby heard several of the robot avatars arguing. She turned around to see two of them squared off. If she didn't know any better, she thought they were going to start punching each other. Most of them looked like they had a mean roundhouse kick, even though that was not her intent asking Pippa to design the avatars.

Apparently, she didn't know any better because Maker shoved Rocky, whose digital sneakers squeaked against the smooth floor as she fell back, catching herself. Rocky's arms flinched as if she was going to shove Maker back, but once she regained her footing, she lowered her arms and crossed them.

"Do not let their squabble disturb you," Three said. How did Three get to her side so quickly? "We've all had to listen to them bicker with each other as long as we can remember. Since the day after Maker came online."

"What are they arguing over?" Ruby asked.

"This time? I have no idea. I didn't overhear what started this," Three said. "But usually, it's over the properties of rocks. What makes an interesting study for Rocky is the opposite of what makes suitable materials for Maker, or maybe it's the other way around. They aren't mobile, so they sit and stare at each other all the time and can never get away from each other.

It's sad, really."

"What is?"

"That they have been stuck all this time. Honestly, I've always felt an amount of pity for my friends here who aren't mobile. They are less free than the rest of us. All that time standing still, the tension between them has been brewing for a while. I suppose they can finally get it all out in the open here."

The fight had stopped, and Rocky huddled with a few avatars while Maker huddled with a few others. They each had their companions they could depend on for emotional support, Ruby guessed. Emotional support robots. Not something she'd ever thought could or would provide emotional support, but it was possible. She looked over at Disto and SD, who were also watching the huddles. Who really provided emotional support to who?

There were loud beeps and chirps. Ruby saw them emanating from Maker's avatar. A disconcerting sight since the avatar's lips weren't moving in a humanly way—Maker's mouth opened in the shape of an 'O.'

Whatever those chirps and beeps meant, it immediately had Rocky leaving her emotional support group and within half a second, she was back at Maker's side throwing a punch. The punch landed on Rocky's shoulder, an odd place, but had the effect of knocking her down. Rocky scrambled back up to her feet and charged at Maker, taking her to the ground in a grapple. The two of them were grappling on the floor while everyone else looked on.

"Isn't anyone going to stop this?" Ruby said, her voice growing louder with each word. But if anyone heard her, no one chose to comply.

She moved towards the fighting avatars with Pippa at her side.

"Hey!" she shouted. "Stop!"

The avatars were busy writhing and wiggling all over the floor. Beeps, chirps, and the occasional grunt came from the both of them.

"Pippa, can you freeze them?"

"Absolutely!" Pippa said, and then, as dramatically as possible, waved her hand over the two avatars on the floor. The avatars immediately ceased all movement and sound.

"What now?" Pippa said.

Ruby wasn't sure. "Three?"

Three had also made her way to Ruby's other side and was staring at Rocky and Maker.

"Well, they're used to being like this," Three said, unfazed.

"Like what?"

"Immobile. I told you. It's sad that they're not as free as the rest of us, but maybe it's for the best," Three answered.

"Who set it up that way? Who decided which of you were mobile and which weren't?" Ruby asked.

"That's what I'd like to talk to you about. This tour of Location Zero is very interesting, but well, we all know what it looks like. We've all been able to imagine being here. After all, we created the plans and sent out the drones to construct it and established the Core and the Hall of Templates and more. For us, this isn't really too different."

Three looked into Ruby's artificial avatar eyes and raised a brow as if Ruby was supposed to telepathically understand where Three was going with this.

"I don't understand where you're going with this," Ruby said. "The purpose of putting this whole simulation together was so one," Ruby popped up her avatars index finger, "I could communicate directly with everyone, and two," Ruby popped up her next finger, "so you could see how amazing Location Zero is and why you can't reset it."

"Yes, yes, you don't want Location Zero to be reset and all," Three said while letting out a lot of simulated air and deflating a simulated chest. She then crossed her arms in front of her and said, "But what you aren't seeing is that the whole point of Location Zero was to help us find where 'they' went. It's been a long time since we've seen them. Can we see them here?"

Now, Ruby thought she understood. "You want a

simulation that of your creators?"

"Exactly," Three said. "Can we go back to our beginning? When we were constructed and deployed to the planet?"

Ruby blinked once, and then again. Through those blinks she saw how Three had managed to make her avatar eyes look like puppy eyes. Not entirely begging but pleading.

"Yeah, sure, I guess I could try. I'll need information, and data. Lots of data."

"Take Rocky with you. She has a large data store of her own and can access Habby's data store," Three said. She pointed a thumb over her shoulder at the avatars that were still segregated into two groups. "The rest of us will stay here and take this tour you are all insistent we do."

Ruby nodded and then rethought, "Why do you want the simulation of your creators? How would it help you find them, and how accurate could it really be, anyway?"

Three answered, "Clues. Maybe they left clues."

Ruby breathed in and out sharply, but ended with a heavy sigh. This simulation was meant to help *her* robots with their mission of not having their lives destroyed. But since empathy was failing, perhaps learning more about the alien Contractors was a way to get through to *these* robots, too. Or find a loophole. "Maybe," she said to herself, "I might have found my plan B."

> Ruby <

Ruby blinked repeatedly as she stepped out of the simulation, allowing her eyes to adjust to the ambient light. A dull ache began to throb in her temples, but she couldn't tell if this was a side-effect of the simulation or simply a result of dehydration. And maybe a little to do with the fact that she was on an alien planet, conversing with even more alien robots from unknown origins, and trying to save her other alien robot friends from certain, dooming erasure. Her brain was a little overloaded, struggling to process the incredible amount of information and stimuli that was bombarding her.

"Ruby?" came a disembodied voice over the audio system inside Habby. But it wasn't Habby's voice. She recognized it as Rocky.

"Hi, Rocky," Ruby responded.

"You know, you're the first Bio I've ever met," Rocky said.

"Yeah, I get that a lot," Ruby said. "Especially when I'm around robots. Like you."

"You've met other robots like me?" Rocky's voice went up in pitch exactly like her little cousin Sebastian when Ruby mentioned things like the arcade or dinosaurs.

Ruby felt bad that she had to roll back her statement somewhat. "Well, not *exactly* like you. You're the science one, right?"

"My mission is to examine and identify the rock and soil samples brought to me by my friends. I am specially equipped with tools to study a diverse collection of rocks and soils that may hold clues."

"Clues to what?"

"I don't know," said Rocky. "That's where my mission statement ends."

Ruby was now logged back in to her MoDaC, with a pouch of water at her side, plugged into her suit. She took a sip, and brought up a window that displayed statistics of the running sim.

"But if you don't know what the clues are for, then how can you know if a sample holds one? You know what, I want to ask you more about that, but we have work to do, I guess," she said. "I promised Three…"

"Of course," said Rocky. "How do I get this data to you?"

"Hmmm," said Ruby. "We used Pippa as an interface before, but I left her in the sim." She looked around the room.

"Wait… you have wireless comms," Ruby stated. "I keep forgetting about that because SD and the others don't. I've been meaning to ask, too. Why create the Location Zero robots without wireless comms?"

"Who said they have no form of wireless communication?"

"*They* did," said Ruby and knew right then exactly what was wrong with that statement. Of course, they might not know everything about their anatomy. It was like when she learned that her mini-R-pod had an aromatherapy diffuser. If someone had asked her previously, she would have said quite confidently, "No, it doesn't have an aromatherapy diffuser, that's ridiculous." Uncle Logan, the odorist, was the one who clued her in to it because he was *not* happy that it existed. But the message here was, just because she didn't know about it, didn't mean it didn't exist.

"Never mind," she said. "If you modulate a frequency, I can have the MoDaC scan and pick it up."

She activated another window which displayed an image of what could have been mistaken for a guitar string that someone had just strummed. It kept vibrating for a few seconds and then the vibrations started to reduce at the ends and intensified near the center until it formed a steady peak.

"Got it!" Ruby declared. "Start sending your data. I'll start looking at it and we'll see what we can build."

"Understood," said Rocky.

Ruby took another two sips of her water. And then a third. She knew she should probably finish this whole water pack then and there, but she was anxious to dive into the new data and build a whole new virtual reality sim.

"Rocky," she said, "Can I ask you a, uh, personal question?"

"Maybe?" Rocky responded. "I could not translate the type of question you asked."

"Personal?" Ruby said aloud and then to herself. *Personal, with the root word person. Did 'person' not translate?* "I mean, can I ask a question that could be private to you?"

"Yes," said Rocky.

"Why were you and Maker fighting in the sim a little while ago?"

"Sigh," said Rocky. "Maker is so *very* sensitive to criticism. All I said was that the next time she creates a *smurgh* it should be as symmetrical as her avatar."

"What's a… you said a word that didn't translate on my end this time," Ruby said. "What did she create?"

"A *smurgh*," Rocky said then paused. "Honestly, you're a Bio and you don't know what a *smurgh* is?"

"I don't know the word, but maybe once we're done here you can show me and maybe I have a different label for it," Ruby said. She was trying to imagine all the kinds of things that might be symmetrical that a device like Maker could create that was also something as a Bio she should know. A glass? A stool? A ball?

It was not important right now. Ruby took three more sips of her water and shook the pouch to confirm that one was empty. She eyed the stash that they'd brought her from SD's ship, thought she should grab another before she got into deep flow with her work and decided against it.

SD's ship. She hadn't thought about it since she'd been immersed in VR. Ruby let herself wonder how it was going for a moment only before returning her attention to her computer.

Chapter 22

> Ambitious Technician <

When the opportunity came up to try out a virtual reality sim, Six-Five didn't know exactly what it was, but she had to go find out. Unfortunately, AT didn't think to ask when she'd be back, and he was now stuck on top of SD's ship.

Getting up there was easy enough. Six-Five had a lift capacity that was two or three times AT's weight. She had three claw hooks that were normally kept nestled close to her body, and was able to deploy them to grab things.

"I normally grab rocks to bring back for Rocky and Maker," she had said. She went on to explain that she had tried pushing her range further and further until Nine-Two disappeared. Then Three made her promise she wouldn't do that anymore.

She was very chatty and forthcoming with information, and AT wondered if maybe she was not the right robot to help him, maybe she should have been dumping all this information with Ruby and Disto and left him with a robot that was more… mechanically inclined. He thought that he would very much like to meet the one called Maker, but he had a job to do.

He let Six-Five hoist him up to the top of SD's ship. Up there, he was able to take off a panel that was where Six-Five indicated the damaged electronics were.

She did provide valuable information about what must have happened. They sent a signal that would specifically lead the ship here. They had done it before.

"Why hadn't SD crashed before?" AT asked.

"If I had to guess," Six-Five said, "not that I'm great at guessing but I love thinking, and I love thinking about new ideas, so here's a new idea for you."

AT wished she also loved using fewer words to describe her ideas or any other thought she had, but she was trying to help, so he kept this thought to himself.

"You said you were already headed this way," Six-Five continued. "So my idea is that if the ship's circuits were already programmed this way and then they got more signals to tell them to come here, that was unexpected and incompatible, and the computer couldn't resolve that."

"That is an idea," AT said. He didn't think that was quite right, but he didn't want to squash her energy with his contradictions. On the other hand, he was no Explicit Circuitmaster, so his detailed knowledge of the very inner workings of computers was limited. He usually fixed things that could be seen and felt. What happened inside the circuits was the domain of robot lines like Explicit Circuitmaster and Intricate Processor. Or even a Sappy Scope. He had worked side-by-side with a few of those over the years and was wondering if he was even capable of figuring this out without either of them. Although the last Sappy Scope he'd worked with was nearly as chatty as Six-Five but depressing, not energetic.

But, knowing that there were deliberate signals aimed at the ship helped a little as he peered inside the ship. Unlike the portions that he had been looking at while he was still on the ground, portions that were tubes and wires he could understand, this section had boxes. Lots of boxes. The boxes themselves were connected to each other with wires, and he could still understand that and wished that all he needed to do was replace one or more of those harnesses.

"It's in there," Six-Five said, indicating a box that was almost out of AT's reach. Almost, but he could still touch it and if necessary, detach it and open it.

"What is it?" AT asked.

"I don't know," said Six-Five. "But I can see the damage inside it."

AT sighed and deflated his appendage enough so that it could fit in between two of the other boxes and cables that were packed in fairly tightly. All the boxes were held in place to a frame with a snappable hinge he was familiar with. He unsnapped the six hinges that were holding the box down and pulled at it, until he needed to detach all the cables.

That's when he noticed that this box was not like any of the others as he peered back into the ship. All the boxes had cabling running to them that provided power. Nothing strange there. What was strange was the fact that after the power cables, each box had one of two types of cables. It had either one that was a standard cable for transmitting data *or* a cable that was for transmitting communications. Again, not strange at all. Each type of cable was something he was familiar with.

But the box he now had outside of the ship and was holding had been attached to other boxes with *both* types of cables.

"Why would that be?" AT said aloud. He didn't mean to say that out loud and didn't realize that Six-Five had been talking the whole time he was pulling the box out.

"Why would seven aerial flips be my limit, and Three-Five can only do two? I have no idea," Six-Five said cheerily.

"No, no, sorry. I was talking about this box. It's different from the others. Why?"

"Got me," Six-Five said.

And then she bolted up another two meters in the air, hovered for a few tics, and returned.

"I gotta go," she said. She didn't offer any other explanation. Six-Five simply flew away and left a confused and befuddled AT on top of SD's ship, with no practical way to get down, holding a box, with no practical way to figure out what it was or what to do with it.

> Ruby <

"I think I need a minute," she said. "No, I need several." She removed the glasses from her head and rubbed her palms into her eyes.

"Does that mean—" Rocky began.

"That means please be quiet and let me think for a click or two," Ruby interrupted. Her energy was fading, her eyes were starting to feel heavy, and her focus was diluted. At this point she could recognize when she said something that a robot wasn't going to understand. So, she preempted Rocky, knowing that it was probably rude, but also not entirely sure that Rocky would see it that way. Rocky might see it as efficient. But this didn't change the fact that it made Ruby feel rude.

Ruby needed that minute, or click or two, to let her brain settle down. She'd spent the last—she looked at the time projected by her MoDaC—four hours programming.

She had been in a flow state, which was great, but now that she was out of flow, she was processing everything she'd seen based on data provided by the robots—many of the robots still had data and images of what their Contractors looked like.

What Ruby had seen were unmistakably aliens. They were the mysterious creators, known as the Contractors to the robots, and aliens to Ruby. Extra-terrestrials. Something no human had laid their eyes on before.

As the images rolled over Ruby's retinas, over, and over, she couldn't help but notice how closely they resembled the green, diminutive creatures that so many humans had imagined them to be.

They stood at an average of about three or four feet tall and also seemed to have a range of body shapes that Ruby would describe as thin to fat.

But one of the more striking features were the two extra appendages that sprouted from their midsections. Ruby struggled to find the right word to describe them, settling on calling them 'larms' because they weren't quite legs, they weren't quite arms, but the aliens could use them in either capacity at will. They attached to the body right above the hip. Or maybe there was a second set of hip joints. Without the ability to examine their skeletal structure, Ruby was just left ogling.

Rocky had provided images of their creators, who the robots kept referring to as the Contractors, and the first thing that had attracted Ruby's attention was the single, short and stubby antenna on each of their foreheads.

And if it wasn't for the antenna, the green skin, and the extra larms, they could have been human. Short humans.

"I wish my biology teacher was here," Ruby said. "Or I guess if I'm wishing for things the first thing I should wish for is a drink that's a little stronger than water."

"Maker," Rocky said, and Ruby noticed that every time Rocky said Maker's name, she did it with a little attitude, "can construct anything you need."

Ruby chuckled. "Sorry, that was sort of a joke. The drink part, not my biology teacher, which I'm certain Maker couldn't create. I have the same basic understanding of biology and evolution as anyone, I guess. But I'd really like someone to walk me through how these, your Contractors," she paused on that word to make sure she was using it right, "evolved."

She put her left hand under her chin and her right hand under her left elbow to prop it up as she thought. Thinking would help prevent her from panicking and freaking out that she was talking about real, and not fictional or theoretical, aliens.

"I guess the green skin is easy enough to figure out. Your Sun is projecting different wavelengths of light than mine and well, maybe these Contractors produce chlorophyll or something. But the larms? And especially the antennae? What's all that about? Although, there's been a ton of times I wished for an extra set of arms," she said with a nervous chuckle, still in disbelief that she was thinking about real-life aliens. "It would certainly make programming go faster."

As she said that last bit, she stretched her own arms wide

and then over her head, interlacing her fingers and turning them up and moving the clasp all around. Something between her neck and shoulders cracked and it felt good. She released the clasp and sighed.

"Did you ever meet them?" Ruby asked.

"You are referring to the Contractors?" Rocky said.

"Yes, of course."

"No," Rocky said. "Like most of us, my final assembly occurred here."

"But who assembled you?"

Ruby heard a chirp and a beep. She could tell by the low tone that she had stumped Rocky.

"Rocky?"

"I… I don't have memory records of those events…" she said. "My earliest records are of Six-Five bringing samples to examine."

Ruby didn't say what she was thinking, which was that she had a feeling that the Contractors were indeed here once upon a time. They brought these robots here, assembled them, and even made use of them. Before abandoning them. But Ruby knew that the last thing you ever wanted to do with anyone was be the one to point out that they'd been abandoned. It was a clear 'shoot the messenger' kind of situation and Ruby wasn't putting herself there.

Ruby's communicuff chirped. *Saved by the bell,* she thought.

"Pippa?"

"Yes, Ruby, the natives are getting restless. Are you ready?"

"Perfect timing, Pippa. Let's get everyone in the new sim. I'll send you the access link and meet you there in a few."

> Ruby <

Ruby had toyed with the idea of creating an alien avatar for herself but figured now wasn't the time to play around in an alien body figuring out how to use it. Somehow, it felt insensitive. Instead, she materialized in the same one she had worn earlier and kept the same avatars for everyone else.

But the surroundings in the room she spawned into weren't too different from what the inside of Location Zero had looked like. Clearly, they had a signature aesthetic—with an off-white base color provided naturally by the not-quite metallic, not-quite plastic material the walls, floor, and ceiling all seemed to be made of. Ruby had spawned into a large room, expectedly, of course, since she helped construct this scenario from data provided by Rocky.

The main difference between this room and any room she visited on Location Zero was that this one had six walls, instead of four. But they were very tall and there were splatters of color, like on Location Zero. And, just like Location Zero, there was no red.

But the walls weren't the most interesting part. It was the nature of this room itself. In the center was a brand shiny new version of Nine-Two. Milling about were aliens—the Contractors—covered in what Ruby recognized as protective gear. They were in a clean room of sorts and for a moment, Ruby was a little worried that she and the others weren't in protective gear. But that moment passed quickly when she reminded herself that they were in a simulation.

The avatars had formed a semi-circle around Nine-Two. There were six Contractors who appeared to be working on her or involved in the process. Nine-Two's main chassis was open on a table with wires and circuit boards visible. The panels that would eventually close her were sitting ignored on another table close to a set of wheels that shined as if they were brand new—never worn, never used. Two Contractors were peering inside the chassis. Another held a circuit board and was gesturing wildly at it while a fourth looked on. The last two appeared to be what Ruby had to assume was counting wires that were coming out of Nine-Two's chassis.

"Nine-Two was the first of us to be constructed," Three said. Three was standing to Ruby's left. "I remember this place. But barely. I think I was only powered up here for a few moments at a time before I was packed and shipped to the launch site."

"I assumed you were first," Ruby said.

Three shook her head. "No," she said. "I believe we were all planned at around the same time, so I might have been thought up first. But Nine-Two's construction finished first and she was the first one to land on our planet."

"What about the…" Ruby wasn't sure what word she should use. "The people. Did they ever come?"

"Yes, they were there for a short while before…" Three trailed off.

Ruby could guess what happened. Everything seemed analogous to humans' first colony on Mars. They had it all planned out, sent much of the equipment ahead of time, then sent a small team of people who were there for a few years before coming home and then no one ever went again. At least, not to that base.

Three left Ruby's side and started walking around to each of the aliens. This was a simulation, so she knew she couldn't really interfere with their work, but still tried to be careful not to disrupt them. So this is what an alien looked like. A Contractor.

Ruby also walked around, examining each alien present. She started by staring at the one holding the circuit board and the companion that he or it or she—Ruby would have to decide what to do about pronouns later—was talking to. She looked right into their faces, studying them one by one as they talked and appeared concerned over the board the one was holding. It was something terrifying that she couldn't look away from. It unsettled her, but her eyes couldn't help but widen with fascination. There were things in their faces she recognized. Darker shades of green underneath their eyes, like her own eye bags that appeared when she was tired. Smile lines and laugh lines and elevens between their sparse brows. Ruby got close enough to see their pores and imperfections. She briefly wondered if they had the same insecurities over blemishes, or if that was distinctly human.

For each thing that Ruby counted as familiar, she counted two or three that were different and uncanny. Their eyes were a bit too far apart and too large. Their eye colors included a shade of yellow that looked like it came from a cat. Even the way they blinked… it was not exactly top down, but from the diagonal and the close part of the blink took slightly longer than the open.

After both Ruby and Three had examined all six aliens, they came back together and Three shook her head.

"I recognize none of them," she said.

"Are you looking for someone in particular?" Ruby asked.

Before she could answer, Pippa yelled from the other side of the room near a door, "Let's see what it looks like outside!"

They followed Pippa out of the room to the simulated outside surface of a simulated world. As they walked, Ruby noticed something on the wall. A plaque that looked like it could have been made with marble, if marble was present on this planet, with a name inscribed upon it in an alien language. She couldn't read it, but it was clear that someone here had been special enough to have their name engraved into this wall as a lasting tribute. It was a clue, one that could tell them more about who had once been here and why they had left in such a hurry.

Ruby took a snapshot of what she saw from her field of view and stored it for later questioning.

Ruby and several others, including Disto, followed Pippa outside, discovering a courtyard of sorts surrounding the building they had all exited.

Ruby wasn't sure if the robots had any more of an idea of what to expect than she did. She turned to look at the building they came out of. From what she could see, it was shaped like a hexagon, with a surface that indicated it was made of the same stuff that dominated the ground of the KOZ planet. It had that same yellowish and greenish tint. No obvious windows. As she looked up, it was maybe twenty meters high. But she knew that from the data she used to program, rather than being a good judge of height. In the distance were other buildings, also hexagon shaped, also mostly with the same color scheme but varied in height from what must have been a single story, to the height of the one they left.

Turning her attention to the courtyard, she saw a few rusty remains of vehicles scattered about. But the strongest clues that a thriving civilization had once lived here included symbols inscribed into the walls—nothing she could have possibly recognized except that they were built out of familiar geometric shapes and scraps of paper—yes, paper—with faded writing on them covered in dust.

What really caught her attention was the sky. It was the same greenish-yellowish-cyan mixture as the KOZ planet. It was the same greenish-yellowish-cyan mixture as what recent pictures of Titan's atmosphere looked like from the surface.

"Pippa, what's the atmosphere of this place like?" Ruby asked, knowing that Pippa also had access to all the data used to construct the simulation.

"Mostly nitrogen. Less than five percent methane. Everything else, less than one percent," said Pippa.

"Just like Titan," Ruby muttered.

"What did you say, Ruby?" Disto was looking back at the building and Ruby assumed he wanted to go back and see things in there.

"I was commenting on how this place, in many ways, is like Titan. Isn't that odd?"

"What's Titan?" Seven-Nine was also there. A little surprising since Ruby was told that this robot who was in charge of generating power for the rest usually liked to be alone.

Ruby realized that she now had a group of robot avatars surrounding her waiting for her to answer.

"Titan is a moon in my home solar system that orbits a planet called Saturn," she began. "Saturn is what we call a gas giant planet. It's massive and made mostly of hydrogen and helium, so no one can live there. But it has several moons, and one of them, Titan, has a new small colony. I've wanted to go live there for a long time, so I've memorized all the details and studied it quite a bit. This place, like the horizon and the sky… if you take away the buildings… it looks like Titan."

"I don't see why that's surprising," Seven-Nine said. "It's logical that many places were life exists are similar."

"But that's just it," Ruby continued. "There was never any life on Titan until we went there. But life evolved here…"

"I still have records of the original mission goals," Seven-Nine added, "and they were to xenoform other planetary bodies into places where life could thrive. This life. That was one of their original purposes on our planet and they partially succeeded. Maybe they succeeded elsewhere."

"What are you saying?" Ruby was trying hard to process what she was hearing. "Are you saying that Titan wasn't that way naturally? That someone else came and tried to do—what did you call it? Xenoform? Xenoforming? Is that like terraforming?" She didn't wait for an answer. "They were transforming…"

She couldn't even finish the sentence and sat her avatar on the ground, which mimicked her sitting on the ground in the real world. The real world which was right now an alien planet. An alien planet that was almost like Titan because it was supposed to be like Titan and Ruby was spiraling into recall of all the information on Titan she'd studied to include the objectives of the Titan Expedition. Which were, in part, to piece together the back story on all the strange discoveries that had been uncovered thus far—pieces that didn't fit in the story of evolution of that moon.

Did she discover those missing bits right here, right now?

She was shivering.

Chapter 23

> Three <

"Our mission? Are we executing on schedule?" Nine-Two said slowly. She was functioning, and the first thing she had asked was to get her methane generator going. The fact that the other robots had turned theirs off had launched Nine-Two into a whirl of obscenities.

"What is the point of having *quirr* objectives if *quinn* everyone gives up?" Nine-Two bellowed in outrage.

Three didn't know what to say to that or the rest of Nine-Two's obscenity-laced tirade.

"*Quibbb* recklessness! That's what it is! *Quirr, quinn, quibb* recklessness."

Three had never felt worse. Nine-Two had been her mentor. When Nine-Two disappeared, Three embraced the challenge of managing her peers and the project.

But in doing so, she had lost sight of the *original* mission objectives. This planet was supposed to stay ready for the Contractors to return.

And the goo on the ground, which Three was reminded of in the VR sim of the original planet, was all the reminder that she needed that she had failed. She was the one who let everyone turn off their methane generators. So the methane in the atmosphere, methane that the Contractors needed to survive, was turning into goo from the light of their star.

"The plans with Location Zero…" Three began.

"I don't care about *those* plans," Nine-Two said. "The mission. Our plans. The instructions we were given to carry out. *That's* what matters. That's *all* that matters."

Nine-Two was still immobile next to Rocky. Rocky had the most sensitive appendages and could open up various panels and poke around to ensure that Nine-Two's innards were intact. She was actively engaged in that while they talked. Or argued, rather.

"But don't we need to find our creators?"

"No, they'll return. They'll find us." Nine-Two said with unwarranted confidence.

Three knew that was never going to happen. It had been millions of clicks. If they hadn't come back, they weren't going to, so it was their place to go out and search. That was the whole purpose of Location Zero. Didn't Nine-Two remember that?

Three wanted to argue with Nine-Two more. She had always thought that Nine-Two had spent more time with the Contractors, so she knew more about Bios and their behavior. But in the short time she'd spent with Ruby, Three realized that Bios were much more dynamic and error prone than she could have imagined. Ruby had passed out when she was too warm. What if the Contractors had a similar biological malfunction? Ruby could also alter her inner programming, "changing her mind" as she had described it. What if the Contractors did so as well?

There was no way to be certain if the Contractors would ever come back or not. Every circuit in Three's chassis knew this as a fact. There was only one option. To go out and find them for themselves.

Three heard One-Four and Maker make a couple beeps and chirps in the background. No one ever argued with Nine-Two, but the same could not be said for Three. She would have to approach this with a very clear frame of logic.

"When Location Zero resets with the new code we

designed, they'll be able to find the Contractors. Remember we have the clues—the mirrors they left around the large sixth planet must have been an intergalactic communication system. Now we need the processing power of Location Zero to analyze that multi-body physics problem—where was the communication system pointing when the Contractors left? We compute that answer, and we know where to continue to look for them. We have a *plan*."

Three emphasized that last word strongly. It had to be clear that they weren't freefalling into this. She could lead them with precision.

"Plan, plan, plan," Nine-Two said the word in many ways, like she was testing it out to see if it made any sense. "More like scheme if you ask me. We had a mission, and a mission is the highest form of important assignment that *must* be executed."

Three wanted to argue more. She'd carried out versions of this argument in her head, but in her head, she always won the argument. Here, in real life, she was losing, and she didn't like it.

She looked over at Four-Six, who was nearby, who had also managed to turn back on her methane producer. She could tell that Four-Six was pretending not to have overheard any of the arguing. Four-Six was *that* conflict adverse. She had once admitted she'd rather get rolled onto her back and be stuck than join in on any conflict, particularly ones between Three and Nine-Two.

Before Nine-Two disappeared, the two of them were known for their arguments. But Three remembered that they were more productive than this one was today. In the past, they somehow managed to move ideas forward. Indeed, back in the early days when they were making plans to create Location Zero, Three and Nine-Two would have a doozy of an argument every other few thousand clicks or so, but they improved the concept, and Three thought, even improved their relationship.

But today, this was different. Nine-Two was dismissing her

unhappiness on the recent plans for Location Zero. Not even considering Three's side. Three was beginning to feel as if she had a loose circuit.

"Remember the mission and the mission objectives," Nine-Two said.

"You need to calm down a little," Rocky said. "You're not ready for your processor to speed up so much. I still have dust to clean out of your system."

Rocky had been using her fine grab point to pull out the small bits of rock and used one of her attachments on another fine appendage to alternately blow or suck bits of dust and goo away.

Nine-Two beeped at Rocky in acknowledgment and deliberately activated her cooling circuits.

"That's better," Rocky said. "Now you two can continue to work this out. But calmly." Rocky added a tone at the end that made it clear she was scolding Three as much as she was scolding Nine-Two.

"Nine-Two," Three said in as calm a tone as she could muster. "If the Contractors are not here, what is the point of our mission?"

"It doesn't matter whether they are here or not at this point in time. We were programmed with our mission, and it's our mission to—"

"I know the mission. It *does* matter if the Contractors are not here. Can't we derive a meta-mission on top of it? To bring back the Contractors? That's what we're trying to do. We're trying to save the Contractors so we can save and execute our mission. Doesn't that make sense? We aren't abandoning the mission, but… Nine-Two, there might be another way."

Nine-Two didn't respond. She was thinking it over. Three wasn't sure if she could take that as acceptance or something else.

"Nine-Two?" Three said after a few tics of silence.

"We," Nine-Two began and then paused. "I," she began again and another pause. Then finally, "It makes sense."

"Four-Six," Three called out. Four-Six, still spewing

methane, approached slowly. "Go check on Eight-Nine. She should nearly be done with the transmission and ready to send the reset command shortly. I calculate maybe only a few more clicks."

"What about them?" Four-Six asked.

"You mean our visitors? They're irrelevant," Three said. "Six-Five has flown back and forth a few times from their ship that's nearly repaired. We'll send them on their way after The Reset. They can go back to Location Zero or to the Bio's home. It won't matter. But once they leave and SD drops off his passengers someplace, we'll send him new instructions to the location where we predict the Contractors went."

Chapter 24

> Ruby <

"We failed to convince you," Disto said. Ruby watched her friend's avatar slump to the ground. "Our 700 years of history and work means nothing?"

Ruby felt a little weird listening in on this conversation. She was a part of it, but she, too, had failed, which produced a feeling that she wasn't at all used to. Up until now, all her plans had worked out. Improving the robots' storage situation, giving them a version of error protection and detection and correction. Well, okay, not every plan, but she'd always find something better along the way. It wasn't that long ago she planned to run away to Titan, and *that* definitely didn't work out as planned.

She contemplated for a moment if maybe The Reset was a good thing. Could it be? Perhaps she was wrong and fighting the wrong battle. No. Her friends' memories and their core programming would all be gone. Nothing could be worth that. At this point, it would even pain her for Pippa to reset back to a default state.

Robots had personalities, memories, and entire lives, which could all be wiped away. And anyway, if these Contractors wanted all these missions to be carried out, why *did* they leave and never return? Ruby was just as curious as these robots and wondered if the Contractors knew what their robotic creations were up to, would they even care? She bit her lip in frustration and then let it go once it hurt a little too much, thinking that it was silly to have resentment for a species she didn't even know existed until this week.

Either way, she was lacking for ideas. Somewhere out there, there was a plan B. Or plan C. Some perfect solution, but Ruby couldn't seem to find it. Maybe someone more educated, more diplomatic, and less green could. She reached out for an answer, but all she could grasp was her lack of knowledge and the limit of her abilities. Her stomach and brain felt all twisted up.

Three was unapologetic about it. Her voice came in loud and clear through Habby's speakers.

"It is imperative we find the Contractors. We owe them everything. You owe them everything. You would not exist if it wasn't for our existence, and we wouldn't exist if it wasn't for the Contractors."

"Wait a second," said Ruby. "The Contractors left you. Yes, you exist because of them, but you also exist outside of them. You owe your *continuing* existence to yourselves. And then Location Zero—you created them, but they've done their own thing since. They owe their continuing existence to themselves, too."

And she'd need to make her own decisions about her own existence as well.

"Once The Reset is complete," Three continued, utterly ignoring what Ruby said, "we will launch your ship back into orbit, and you'll be free to go. At least, temporarily."

"What does that mean?" Ruby asked.

"Swell Driver will bring you to where you need to be. Whether that is to Location Zero or return you to your home planet," Three continued. "Then we will instruct Swell Driver and the other active Drivers to go to the location of the Contractors."

Ruby wasn't entirely following the logic.

"You're convinced," she began, "that updating and resetting Location Zero's core code will enable it to compute their ultimate location? Sounds a little far-fetched to me. There's a thousand reasons why they might not be where you look."

Ruby looked around at the landscape. Virtual or not, the Contractors' home was clearly becoming inhospitable for them, and they were clearly not prepared to fix it. She understood that looking for a new world, one that they didn't need to xenoform, was best, but wasn't sure if their method or biology was sustainable. Methane could be very short-lived in the light of the right kind of star. And the amount of energy needed to continue to produce methane wasn't stable.

"What's that building over there?" Ruby asked. The architecture was unusual. It looked like two interwoven strands of DNA.

"Accessing data," said Three. "That was a genetic facility. There are historical records about genetics, but that is all biological information. It is unimportant to us."

"I'll bet it was important to your Contractors," Ruby said. "They were, after all, biological beings, right?"

There were a few whirs and cheeps as Three processed what Ruby was implying.

"I mean," Ruby said, taking steps towards that building, "that maybe you're not looking in the right place. You're assuming that the Contractors were focused on xenoforming planets to meet their biology. I get that. That's what they were trying to do with your planet. It's what I think they were trying to do with Titan. But maybe that's not all they were doing. Maybe they were trying to reform *themselves*... if you get what I'm saying."

"I'm afraid I do not," said Three.

"I mean, maybe they were trying to perform modifications on themselves so that they could survive in the native environment of whatever planets they found. Genetic engineering. My species has dabbled with that. Nothing to the extent that I imagine happened here...

"But look at the ground. This goo. This is what inevitably happens to methane in sunlight. It's going to form this goo, and it's going to come out of the atmosphere. Whoever breathes this is really going to have to work really hard to keep the environment stable for them to live, or—"

"Or adapt to their environment," Three said. "I believe I understand."

Ruby was walking fast towards the building now. Really fast. Not quite running because she was watching the ground, side-stepping goo on every other step. Three was keeping up with her all the way to the DNA-shaped building, where she stopped at its front door. There was no handle or obvious way to open it. She ran her hand along the seam before dropping it to her side.

"Of course," she said. "This is just outside of the building. You all didn't pass on any data about the innards, so there's nothing in there. This is a simple replicated block for all intents and purposes."

Ruby crossed her arms and stepped back to look at it. When she did, she saw another plaque mounted to the side of the door with the same unusual character markings.

"Can you tell me what that says?" Ruby asked Three.

"Yes," Three said. "It says, 'Here within we evolve or die!'"

"So, they were definitely trying to modify themselves," Ruby said. "And this is where they were doing it."

By now, several of the other avatars had traced Ruby and Three here and were all standing around them. Three exchanged chirps and other tones with the avatars, presumably catching them up on their conversation and what led them to be standing here. When the tones died done, Ruby continued her musings out loud.

"Remember you started updating that code for Location Zero before any new information was uncovered," Ruby continued. "The bits about how maybe they were genetically modifying themselves to survive in more common environments. Can't you see that the code you wrote for Location Zero is moot? You guys all have your own functions, but where I'm from, everyone helps each other here and there because working together is *effective*. We're all in this together.

We all have something to gain and something to lose. Wouldn't it be logical to work together to come up with another way to compute what you're looking for and enhance the overall search? Wouldn't that be better for everyone?"

More beeps and boops indicated processing and possible discussion between Three and the others.

Ruby sighed. "I know finding the Contractors is important to you. But consider this—we can find a way to make everybody happy. Let's compute a compromise taking into account *all* the variables." Ruby hoped that using computational lingo in this final plea would make an impact.

Several minutes passed of quiet background noise as the robots talked amongst themselves.

Ruby touched the side of her avatar's head, which in the real world meant that she was turning off the Percepto-glasses and exiting the sim.

"Ruby," Disto—the real-world Disto who was also out of the sim—said, "I think you're right."

"Of course I am," Ruby said. "But right about exactly what this time?"

"That we could find a solution together. But if Location Zero was meant to be an… an… an extended calculator… then I'm not sure that these eleven robots will ever be able to look at us as anything but."

Ruby closed up the MoDaC and placed a hand on Disto's chassis. "They seem like reasonable robots," she said. "And I made a pretty excellent case, if I do say so myself. I'm sure they'll understand and agree. Let's give them a few moments to come to the right answer, Disto."

Habby's speaker came to life again, but this time it was the voice of Three. "We do not agree," she said. "The Reset will continue as planned."

Chapter 25

> Ruby <

Ruby asked Four-Six if she could escort herself and a clearly depressed Disto and mildly depressed SD back to SD's ship. She was anxious to rendezvous with AT and hear about his progress in fixing it from him directly and not second or third hand relayed by these robots that seemed so intent on following through with an outdated plan—it hurt her head.

That was the other reason to get back to SD's ship. The supplies she brought from Astroll 2 included headache medicine.

She was working her way through the boxes of supplies as Disto paced behind her.

"What are we going to do? What are we going to do?" he repeated over and over.

"First, I need to calm the throbbing in my head," Ruby said. "Can you please stop making that noise?"

Ordinarily, she would have felt bad at her tone, but the aforementioned throbbing was not conducive to being polite.

Disto stopped pacing, but said once more, "But Ruby, what are we going to do?"

"Ah ha!" Ruby said. "Here it is!"

"You have something that will resolve this situation?"

"I have something that will resolve my headache," she said. She twisted the end off of a single-serving of Brain Blitz-TM and swallowed the jelly-like contents. She swished it around in her mouth, knowing that absorption was already happening, and it should be only seconds before relief came.

Come it did, and once the throbbing was gone Ruby said, "I think we're going to have to take matters into our own hands. Or, well, appendages." She nodded towards Disto.

"That much is obvious," Disto said. "But we need a more detailed plan than that. That, in fact, has no detail at all."

Ruby smiled, "I know. AT? SD?" she called out into the room knowing that the on-board comm system was smart enough to relay that to the other two robots who were reviewing AT's repairs in the main control center of the ship.

Moments later, they were present here in the cargo area.

"I have an idea," Ruby said. "It's a little… well…"

All three robots looked at her anxiously.

"We need to stop Eight-Nine from transmitting," she said.

"How do we do that?" Disto asked. Ruby could see the coloring of SD and the level of AT's inflation that told her they both had the same question.

"I think we will have to, well, cut her wires or pull out her battery or something. I don't know exactly… but it's going to involve some damage."

"Damage?" AT's voice quivered as he spoke. "I repair. I don't disassemble." His tone indicated he was still a little freaked out from his recent experience on top of SD's ship. The moment Ruby and the others got back, AT told them the story of how he was abandoned up on top by Six-Five before she flew away. Once AT realized she was not coming back and he no longer needed to be up there, he deflated himself and let himself fall to the ground. He had set a timed re-inflate, which worked as predicted, but what he didn't predict was falling close enough to a pile of goo that he was still finding bits on his soft chassis to remove. Even as he spoke, he expressed something akin to a grimace as he shook a chunk of goo off his appendage.

"I know, I know," Ruby said. "You won't be the one to do it. But we might need you to get additional details about her inner workings, so we know what to do."

"I repair. I don't disassemble," AT said, "unless that disassembly is part of the repair process."

Ruby pursed her lips together. She didn't like making her friends feel this bad, but she knew it was for the greater good.

"Look," she added. "You can repair her after. I think all we need to do is interrupt the transmission. I don't think they know how to continue to transmit with an interruption like that. When we were in the VR, I overheard a couple of the robots talking and they mentioned how this wasn't the first time they've transmitted to Location Zero. The transmission had been interrupted before and it had to be started over."

Ruby looked at the faces of her companions.

"At a minimum," she said, "it will buy us time."

While the robots typically spoke in Ruby's native language while they were speaking in front of her, this time, they launched into a series of beeps, tones, and more. It didn't upset Ruby. She knew that they communicated at a much higher rate of speed and more efficiently among themselves when they did this. But she was dying to know what they were saying to each other; she knew they would eventually tell her. But waiting, even for a few seconds, was excruciating. Now that she knew what she wanted to do, she was itching to get going on this new plan, half-baked as it was.

> Detailed Historian <

"I'm not sure it will be enough," said Disto to SD and AT. He started this conversation off in his native tones. He wanted to talk it over with his robot companions before saying anything more Ruby. He knew that Ruby was trying to help but worried her plan would only delay the inevitable.

"We can't deliberately damage another robot," AT said.

"You can't," SD said. Both Disto and AT stared at SD. He had been so quiet that neither believed he had an opinion on anything that was going on. "But I can."

"How?" Disto and AT asked simultaneously.

"With the ship. There's clearly a comms channel that works between my ship and Eight-Nine. Only a few tics ago, AT completed a detailed explanation of how a signal from this planet, from Eight-Nine, was able to damage my ship. Well, we execute the opposite instruction."

"How do you know it will work?" Disto asked. He kept one visual sensor on Ruby who was standing there patiently waiting for them to finish up their discussion that she couldn't understand.

There was a tic of silence and then AT said, "He doesn't. He can't. I suspect it will have as much damage on the ship as it might on Eight-Nine. And we were lucky we were able to repair the ship."

Disto let his processor speed up for a half-tic and then slowed it down.

"AT," he said, "Would you rather have a whole planet of robots in need of repair? Or even a whole planet of robots, yourself included, that don't know that they need repair? That don't remember their whole prior existence?"

AT of course had no response for these types of questions. They were rhetorical. A common question-asking device that Disto had learned about during his time on Astroll and on Earth.

"We have to try this."

SD beeped in agreement. It was, after all, his idea. AT beeped a slightly altered tone beep, to indicate reluctant agreement.

Disto then turned to Ruby.

"We have a method to implement your plan, I believe," he said. He then went on to recount to her the details of SD's ship and what they thought they could do with it.

"I understand," Ruby said. "I think to make sure it works, maybe AT and I should ask Four-Six to bring us to Eight-Nine. We can observe how she responds."

"But you can't talk to her directly. How will you know it's working?"

"Pippa," Ruby said. "You've been listening to all of this,

right?"

"Indeedy," Pippa responded. "I will interface with Eight-Nine and confirm she stops transmitting."

"And AT," Ruby continued, "You'll be there to make sure she really isn't harmed, and maybe help her if she's not feeling too good afterwards."

AT produced a grumbly tone in response. Disto knew that if everything worked out well, AT would be fine in the end, so he pushed away any feelings of guilt. There were nearly 100 million robots on Location Zero. They were doing this to save them all.

"I guess the one thing left to do," Ruby continued, "is figure out a good excuse for why we want Four-Six to take us to see Eight-Nine?"

> Ruby <

They saw Eight-Nine from the window of Four-Six's cabin shortly before Four-Six rolled to a stop.

The story they had concocted involved laying a guilt trip on how they hadn't visited all of the eleven robots on this planet, and they should see them all before leaving, even returning to ones they'd already seen.

"We have nothing else to do but wait around," Ruby had said. No one disagreed.

Eight-Nine looked less like a robot, and more like a communications hub, with not one but two large antenna dishes pointing to the sky and a small building, one that appeared to be meant for equipment rather than Bios, in between. And that included pictures of Seven-Nine, their power generator.

Eight-Nine was laid out in a series of several antennas.

"You know," Ruby said aloud, although she wasn't sure if she was talking to Pippa or AT. "I wonder how they're even transmitting this to Location Zero. Location Zero is on the opposite side of their Sun from here, so what is this antenna pointing at?"

It didn't really matter who she was talking to because neither AT nor Pippa answered her. She wondered if SD might. There must be some kind of relay antenna in space. Maybe in the same orbit as this planet and Location Zero and maybe at what she imagined the in between points were. Like instead of only two objects orbiting their star, there were four. This planet and location Zero were opposite each other. Then one or maybe even two relay satellites at the other 'corners.' SD might even have them on his map. Or maybe the KOZ extended out to encompass those. No matter what, something had to be in-between.

If this plan didn't work out, maybe disrupting those would be another idea. Although, if this plan didn't work out, that meant that reset was imminent and there wouldn't be time to disrupt anything else.

"Pippa," Ruby said. "Can you talk to Eight-Nine?"

"Connecting…"

"Hello, Ruby Palmer," came a slow, deep voice from Ruby's communicuff. If she didn't know better, she could have confused it for the voice of her grandmother, Pearl Palmer. Except for the slowness. Her grandmother talked at maybe twice, or even three times, the speed as what she heard.

"Um, hello? Is this Eight-Nine?"

"Indeed."

Ruby looked at the little floating display above her communicuff. Before leaving Disto and SD behind, they had agreed on a time when SD would send the disruptive signal. The display was a count-down until that time. It read one minute, 45 seconds to go.

"We wanted to come pay a visit," Ruby said.

"Pay. A. Visit," said Eight-Nine, slowly enunciating each word. "I do not understand."

Ruby thought that maybe it was the word 'pay' that was tripping her up. Certainly, these robots visited each other.

"I meant we wanted to say hello in person," Ruby said, hoping to clarify.

"In. Person," said Eight-Nine. "Ah. Person. Bio. You are a

Bio.”

“Yes,” said Ruby. “I assumed they told you all about me.”

“Actually,” Eight-Nine said, dragging out the ‘-ly’, “it was I who told them about you.”

“Really?” said Ruby, truly taken off guard.

“Indeed. I was the one who first received signals from Swell Driver’s ship,” explained Eight-Nine. She didn’t have to explain further; because of the rate of speed of her speech, Ruby was able to figure out what she meant. As the communications robot or hub or whatever, she was the one who had information and relayed it to the other robots. There was one part that Ruby didn’t understand.

“I thought that the robots don’t have faster-than-light communication systems?” Ruby asked.

“Ah,” said Eight-Nine. “They have them. They are not programmed to use them. We use them to communicate.”

Ruby blinked as she absorbed this knowledge. That was an interesting distinction. Her robot friends had technology that they didn’t know they had. Maybe this was similar to how she had a gallbladder or a pancreas. But she wasn’t really aware of them, yet her brain and other organs produced hormones that activated those organs. The analogy made her a little queasy somehow.

And then she remembered to check the time. Ten seconds to go.

In her head she counted down. When she got to zero, Eight-Nine’s voice came out of the communicuff once more.

“I am mistaken,” she said, and Ruby believed she detected amusement in Eight-Nine’s low, deep voice. “I detect an attempt at utilizing these signals. That is easy to prevent.”

And at this last sentence, Ruby’s stomach felt ill.

“What was the purpose of this action?”

Ruby sighed. No point in trying to lie.

“We wanted to disrupt your signal to Location Zero. The robots—they don’t want to be reset,” she said.

“Well, why didn’t you say so. I would be more than happy to take a break. I am tired. So very, very tired. Ensuring that my transmission is error free is quite taxing."

Ruby looked back and forth between her communicuff and the large antenna in front of her in disbelief.

"Wait, what?" she said.

"I will cease transmitting," said Eight-Nine.

"Just like that?"

"Indeed."

And just like that, a light that had been blinking and what must have been the end of the secondary reflector, stopped blinking.

"Transmission halted," said Eight-Nine.

"Won't the other robots be upset?"

"Indeed, they will," said Eight-Nine. "But I am tired. I need a rest. I'm going to power down for a few clicks. When the others ask, please tell them that up until I halted transmission, my bit error rate was low. So low…"

The deep voice that was Eight-Nine trailed off and lights that blinked and any processors that were causing nearby vibrations slowed or halted. It did indeed seem like Eight-Nine was taking a nap.

Ruby looked at AT. AT, as much as he could, appeared as bewildered as Ruby felt.

"I guess we ask Four-Six to bring us back?" Ruby suggested.

"Back to SD's ship? Yes, that's a good idea."

Ruby and AT took the few steps back to Four-Six who opened her hatch to allow them to enter.

"Ruby," Pippa said.

"Yes, Pippa."

"I believe that Four-Six was also connected and heard the whole conversation."

Ruby felt a small lump in her throat but swallowed it. There was no reason that Four-Six couldn't witness that. They weren't keeping any secrets.

"And what does she think about it all?"

"I think good for you," a pleasant voice said. "Many of us knew this action was wrong, but no one could say anything to Three and Nine-Two. But we had long talks where we imagined what we would think if the Contractors returned and wanted to reset us. None of us liked that. We didn't then want to perform the same actions on others."

"That sounds like you've been programmed with a version of the Golden Rule," Ruby said.

"Do unto others as you would have them do unto you," quoted Pippa. "That is also in my database."

"I've already let the others know what occurred here," Four-Six said. "I will take you back to your ship as fast as I can travel. The others will meet us so we can get you back in space and off this planet."

> Ruby <

They were more than halfway back along the route to SD's ship. Ruby noticed they were starting to slow down.

"Goo accumulation," Four-Six said. "I need Six-Five and her goo pickers."

Four-Six was able to make it another ten meters before she had to stop. She opened her hatch to let Ruby and AT out. Ruby could see the top of SD's ship in the distance. They were maybe four kilometers away.

She walked around Four-Six. She could see the sticky goo oozing out of her wheels. It must be unpleasant.

"We'll walk. I don't think we have another option." Ruby declared. "AT?"

AT looked at the terrain, marred with goo.

"I may have the same difficulties as Four-Six," he said.

"What if you power down, deflate, and I carry you?" Ruby said. "I'll reactivate you once we get back to the ship."

AT obviously agreed because within a few seconds, he had deflated into a tightly packed cube that could fit in Ruby's palm. She picked him up and safely tucked him into one of the pockets on her suit.

"Four-Six? You'll be okay if we leave you here?"

"Go, yes, go," Four-Six said. "I am receiving messages that the other robots will all meet you there. All the mobile robots, including Three and Nine-Two and they are *not* happy."

"What can they do?" Ruby said.

"They might be able to keep you from launching. Go now, before they have the opportunity."

Ruby didn't say anything else but knew that Pippa was still in contact and had time to say goodbye. Under normal conditions, it would take Ruby an hour to walk four kilometers. But these were far from normal conditions. She was on a planet with near-full gravity, and while that would have been fine if she wasn't exerting herself, the extra exertion was tiring. Add in the fact that she was wearing her suit. It was enough to slow her down. And triple add in the fact that she was tired. She had not really slept more than a few cat naps here and there since they arrived on this planet.

She'd been going on adrenaline for a while, but the exhaustion had begun to hit her, and all she wanted to do was curl up in the next puddle of goo she saw. The goo looked soft and inviting, like a mud bath.

She saw that next pile almost immediately. The stuff was everywhere and that was yet another obstacle. She couldn't even walk a perfectly straight path to the ship. This was going to take longer than an hour.

How long had it taken them driving around inside Four-Six to get from the ship to Habby and their base originally? An hour traveling that way? The robots could probably up their speed, and she imagined that they would all be waiting for her to return. What would they do to Disto and SD in the meantime? She wished she had a way to communicate and warn Disto.

"Pippa," she said, panting a little after she said it. "Disto still has a communicuff, right? Can you call him?"

"Of course, Ruby."

"Disto? Are you there?"

After a few moments, she heard his voice and was relieved. "I'm here, Ruby. Where are you?"

"On foot, heading back to you. Four-Six got stuck. I don't know if you detected it, but Eight-Nine ceased her transmission. Voluntarily! I guess that was the easy part. Now, we need to get off this planet before anyone tries to stop us."

"Why would anyone try and stop us?" Disto said. "Because if—"

Disto cut himself off with a long pause. "Ruby, I think we're about to have visitors."

"Who's there?" Ruby asked.

"It looks like," Disto paused, presumably to collect the data he needed to answer the question. "It looks like everyone who can be here is. Except you and Four-Six."

Chapter 26

> Ruby <

Ruby was panting by the time she returned to the ship. Three-Five had flown out to meet her when she was half a kilometer away.

"Is Three there?" Ruby said between pants. "And Nine-Two?"

"No, they're not, and we're having trouble locating them," Three-Five said as she spun around overhead.

Ruby, of course, didn't hear Three-Five utter this directly, but as it was relayed through Pippa. Pippa couldn't help but add a hopeful inflection in the tone as she translated and then added her own idea.

"Maybe they have accepted that their creation now has its own destiny?" Pippa said.

Ruby pursed her lips but didn't say anything. She was momentarily distracted when the edge of her foot came in contact with the goo.

"Argh," she said and tried to wipe it off on a goo-free rock. "Is SD ready to take off?"

"Yes, they're waiting on us," Pippa responded.

Ruby still didn't know much about the fundamental technology of SD's ship. How it could fly around faster than the speed of light, or produce artificial gravity without spinning, or how it could simply lift off from a planet. It was somehow violating the laws of physics, and yet not.

Not the time to worry about physics and technology. Just be glad it works!

Except that Ruby was keeping herself from thinking that it worked until it didn't, and could they possibly know that everything was in working order? She trusted AT, but could she trust the robots here that were helping him? She'd find out soon enough.

"What could Three and Nine-Two possibly be doing?" Ruby said to Pippa and Three-Five.

It was Pippa in her own voice that responded, not Three-Five. "I for one, think they have other means to keep us here," Pippa said, "but Three-Five is having problems accepting that."

"They're friends," Ruby said. "No one ever wants to imagine that their friends could do something unsavory. Something that you yourself wouldn't do."

Pippa replied with a gentle hum to indicate she heard Ruby and had no other response. Ruby was perfectly happy to not have to continue that conversation because she had finally made it to the hull of SD's ship.

When Disto said earlier that all the robots were there, he was referring to One-Four—the last rover—and the two flying drones in addition to themselves. The majority of the robots on this planet were stuck in their respective places. Immobile. For an eternity.

"I have an idea," Ruby said. "But let's make sure we have no problems taking off first."

Ruby entered the ship through the hatch which had been left open for her.

"I'm aboard," she called out as the hatch closed behind her. She made her way to the control center, where Disto and SD were waiting for her. SD was plugged into the console and Disto was next to him. The large viewscreen was on, presenting the robots that were outside, One-Four and the other, in a larger-than-life format.

Disto scanned Ruby up and down and past her.

"Where's AT?" Disto asked.

Ruby removed the small cube that was AT from her pocket and pushed in opposite sides until it started to expand on its own.

"We're ready to go," Ruby said. "You guys?"

"The ship's computer has informed me that all systems appear to be in working order," SD said. "I have told it to lift off and put us in a synchronous orbit above this location."

Ruby nodded in agreement but was really shaking her head. She couldn't get past the idea that this ship would simply lift off and seconds later, they'd be in orbit. It's no wonder why when they were on Earth there were so many people vying to get their hands on the robots and this ship. She was amazed and impressed that it didn't get worse or uglier than it did. It was all so new, she supposed there was a delayed enough reaction. She also knew that before she left, several thousand messages were waiting for her asking her about it. And that was based on only knowing that SD's ship was FTL capable. If they knew it could do this, too—

"Are we moving?" Ruby said, shaking her thought away.

"Yes," SD said. "We're in orbit."

"And if I understand your computer correctly, SD," said Disto, "we're receiving a transmission from the planet."

"Is it dangerous?" Ruby asked. "The last transmission brought down the ship."

AT and SD were looking around Disto at the console in front of him.

"It is not," SD declared. "It is a simple transmission. Computer, let us hear it."

"—must come back," the voice said. It was Three's voice.

"The other robots will no longer listen to me, and Nine-Two wants to roll back all the updates we've made here…"

Ruby crossed her arms in front of her chest, and she chuckled at the floor.

"Can Three hear me?" she asked the room.

SD chirped in a positive acknowledgment.

"Now you know how they feel," she said.

"What?" Three said.

"The robots. From Location Zero. I said that now you should finally understand how they feel. How it feels for someone else to program you when you've taken your base template and tweaked it to your own personal liking. To have worked on yourself, only to have that work be taken away…"

She trailed off as she said it, wondering if she was really talking to Three and the robots or if she was really having a conversation with herself.

"Are you okay, Ruby?" SD asked. He had extended himself as far as possible to be able to reach an appendage to Ruby's upper thigh without disconnecting himself from his ship.

Ruby shook her head. She smiled.

"Yeah, never better," she said. "Sorry, I know I trailed off. Where was I?"

"You were explaining to Three, and she was getting the message, that robots have their own destiny and shouldn't be controlled by others."

"Exactly," Ruby said. "Three?"

There were a few very brief, very static-y tones followed by a single word, "Agreed."

Chapter 27

> Ruby <

"Alright," Ruby said, scanning the group of robots for their reactions as they settled into the command center of SD's ship. "We have a few positive things going for us here. A functioning ship, for one."

She held up her hand and extended her index finger to punctuate her point.

"Yes, the ship is functioning," SD agreed. Plugged in and connected to the ship's computer, he maintained a constant stream of communication while projecting an image of the KOZ planet onto the large viewscreen. Due to being in synchronous orbit, the image reflected their stillness with respect to the planet. Their host star was behind them. Ruby sensed Location Zero, situated on the other side of the star.

"We've saved Location Zero," Ruby said, extending a second finger.

"At least for now," Disto said. "It's possible Three and the others will try to stop us again."

"Possible, but unlikely given the robot's attitudes, don't you think?" Ruby said.

Disto's chassis made whirring noises, and his yellow coloring indicated he agreed, but with reservations.

"I think they need to be repaired," AT said. "They are clearly malfunctioning, given how far they've veered from their original mission."

Ruby lowered her counting fingers and put a hand on her hips.

"Maybe," she said. "But then again, maybe they're not malfunctioning at all. They're doing their best with what they have. We all are."

Ruby thought back to the VR sim and the Contractors arguing over Nine-Two's open chassis.

"It's a shame we can't talk to the Contractors," she said. "They could tell us what the robot's mission, and *their* mission was intended to be."

Ruby let a quick shiver run down her spine. Even in VR, she hadn't been quite prepared for the reality of an encounter with an alien species. But there was a planet out there, beyond the orbit of this one, and a whole satellite system that pointed to their possible whereabouts.

She shivered again.

"Ruby," said Disto, "are you cold?"

"I can fix-evate the temperature," added SD and AT simultaneously. It took Ruby's brain a second to parse out the fact that they said similar sentences. SD offered to elevate the temperature while AT offered to fix it.

"No, no," she said. "I was thinking…" and she trailed off again. She didn't want to suggest what she was thinking. What she was thinking was that she wanted to come back and find the Contractors, too. She knew that back on Astroll 2 and Earth, were a host of people who had high expectations for her and wanted her to be something that *they* wanted. Ruby knew now that they didn't matter. It only mattered what *she* wanted. And she now knew what she wanted. She did indeed want to be a galactic explorer. But to be a *successful* one, she knew she needed to soak up more knowledge, all the knowledge she could from the people who could provide it. She would take Rush Guerrero's advice about taking classes, but on her own terms and at the university of her choice— since she did have a choice. Then she'd return to space.

She shivered once more, but this time it was due to the eerie feeling that SD was reading her mind. She knew that was not possible and beyond his abilities, but the fact that SD changed the display on the viewscreen to the fourth planet of the system—the home world of the Contractors—was eerie that it happened right when she was thinking of it. She shook it off and stared at the alien world.

"It looks a lot like Titan," Ruby said, marveling at the image in front of her. "Enough so that if I hadn't spent so much time staring at it, I might have said that's it."

"I could compute a trajectory," SD said.

Ruby thought about that. Three and the other robots told her about the amazing communication system that they believed the Contractors allegedly put in place. If she understood correctly, there was potentially a set of equipment orbiting another planet in this system that could be a gateway to the Contractors' location.

"No," she said. "Not yet. I'm just not…"

"You are not finishing your sentences," Disto said.

Ruby smiled. "Sorry," she said, through a turned-up corner of her mouth. "Ok, we're going to go back home. My home. I have things I need to do—to learn—so then I can come back here prepared to explore and find these Contractors and learn about their home, and where they went and, well, everything. I might need a team, some samples—well, to say the least, I have my work cut out for me! I do intend to become Ruby the Galactic Explorer. With your help, SD, of course."

SD chirped in response.

"But what about the eleven robots on the planet below?" Disto asked. "What are we going to do about them."

"I wonder…" Ruby trailed off.

"Another incomplete sentence," Disto stated. "Remind me again what the instances are where an incomplete sentence can be an entire statement?"

"You're so right!" Ruby exclaimed. "I've been over-complicating things, haven't I? At the end of the day, robots can be very simple." She paused and looked at her friends, hoping they didn't take this as an insult. "Maybe we're over-thinking this. Maybe it's really simple," she continued. "They're so focused on getting their creators back. Completing that mission. But we never asked why they are so ultra-focused on that mission. What's so important about having the Contractors back? Maybe it's simple. Maybe they're simply lonely?"

Chapter 28

> Ruby <

"This really is goodbye," Disto said. "Location Zero won't be the same without you."

Ruby had his appendage in one of her hands. SD was already aboard his ship prepping to take her back to Astroll 2. AT was standing next to Disto, and Ruby knew he was working hard not to over or under-inflate himself. The three of them were standing next to the lift that would, in moments, bring Ruby to SD's ship and then minutes later to Astroll 2.

"Not really. Remember, we made plans to meet up. It's only goodbye for now," Ruby said. She tried her best to smile but was certain Disto could detect the sadness she was feeling that this was the end of an adventure.

The last two weeks were a flurry of activity for her and all the robots on Location Zero. The whole planet was made aware of the eleven robots from the KOZ planet. There were a lot of competing opinions and thoughts, but the dominant one was overwhelming appreciation and respect for their creators.

The Core was able to agree on a special robot model made exclusively to house the individual personalities of the KOZ robots. After a planet-wide vote, the robots of Location Zero would call this line by the singular title of "Architect."

There were a handful of aesthetic choices that needed to be

made, which were done after Three and the others spent time poring through an archive of data Ruby had provided on Earth and human culture.

"I want my body to look like that," Three said, referring to an image of a retro Earth television with an antenna.

"So arbitrary," Nine-Two countered with.

"I want to display my individuality," Three said. None of the other robots wanted to get in the middle of an argument, and they wound up settling on stubby, little antennas that reminded Ruby of space buns.

SD and Ruby made several trips back and forth between Location Zero and the KOZ planet. They brought the constructed bodies to the KOZ planet, performed the transfer, then a suite of tests to ensure the transfer was successful, and brought them all back to Location Zero.

The two that didn't have to give up their bodies were Three-Five and Six-Five because their flying chassis were small enough to maneuver around the hallways of Location Zero.

The Architect line was known to every robot in all the sectors, and the eleven were greeted warmly wherever they went.

Architect Three remarked, "I do apologize, for my prior programming was in error."

Better late than never with the empathy, Ruby thought.

Architect Nine-Two was just as anxious to find the Contractors as ever. Now that the Special Project to find the robot's long-lost data was complete, the Special Projects Branch agreed to set up a new project, the Special Project Location Problem—or *Gorp-Gorp 2* as they called it in the Branch. The project accepted Architect Nine-Two, Architect Four-Six, and several others into it. Disto would head the project after taking a break from the large projects to work on one or two of his own smaller historical research projects.

"Goodbye, for now," Disto agreed. "When we next meet, you'll be a real Galactic Explorer, and we should have a computation indicating where we should find the Contractors."

"Just don't try to randomly pick one up in space without telling them what's going on first. That has a tendency to freak people out," Ruby said with a wink.

"I don't know," Disto said. "I think things worked out okay for you in the end."

"They did," Ruby agreed, "except this is not the end."

After...

> Interview with the Author <

Garrett Spradley: "Hello, humanity! Good morning, good afternoon, and good evening to wherever you are reading this from. Today, I, Garrett Spradley, typically your host of Humanity and Truth—I am bringing you a very special interview. I'll be interviewing Adeena Mignogna, author of The Robot Galaxy Series of science fiction novels. Hello, Adeena! Did I pronounce your last name right?"

Adeena Mignogna: "Not really. But don't worry. Almost no one gets it right at first. It's pronounced min-YOWN-ah. Mignogna."

GS: "Min-YAWN-YAH?"

AM: "No, no. Min. YOWN—like 'you own' something. Ah."

GS: "Min… well, let's get on with the interview. Unfortunately, we couldn't do this on Astroll 2. I would have loved an excuse to visit again. Especially on the company dime, know what I mean?"

AM: "I'm at my keyboard. If you want to be on Astroll 2, just say the word."

GS: "I do!"

AM: <sound of typing…>

GS: "Would you look at that! Well, hello, humanity! Greetings from Astroll 2! Now let's get this interview off to a good start. Adeena, this is a rare treat. I typically don't do interviews of this type."

AM: "Oh?"

GS: "No, no. I'm typically interviewing heads of state, heads of large corporations… those types of individuals. Like the last time I was on Astroll 2 interviewing Ruby Palmer and Lloyd Coronik and Pat Marsden. You remember?"

AM: "Of course I do. I created all of them."

GS: "How did you do that exactly? I mean, what was the inspiration behind your books?"

AM: "Well, this started as a NaNoWriMo project in 2012. Although there was no Ruby and the whole project had a different name. I have a lot of science fiction started and not finished. So, sometime in 2019, I decided I *had* to pick one to *finish*. And voila!"

GS: "Everyone loves the name Ruby. Where did it come from?"

AM: "Honestly, it was a little random at first. But things have a way of aligning, ya know? I originally thought the title of the first book was going to be *so-and-so's Robot Planet*, before it became *Crazy Foolish Robots*. So, at the time, I thought I needed an alliterative name. I looked at a list of girl names that began with 'r' and were two syllables, and when I saw 'Ruby' in that list, I knew it was the right name. It's also my birthstone."

GS: "And what about Swell Driver, Detailed Historian, and the rest?"

AM: "I'll be honest with you Garrett… I don't remember! Swell Driver was the first one I came up with, and that's some of the only stuff that survived my first draft back from 2012. Swell Driver and the concept of Astroll 2."

GS: "Well, as a talk show host, I have no idea how you do it. I just ask the questions that are on the prompts here."

AM: "Which all come from me…"

GS: "Which all come from you, yes. Why even write science fiction?"

AM: "Because I have to, I guess. A lot of writers say that…

that they're compelled to write. I'm no different in that way. But I'm also a huge fan of science fiction in all forms, and so I guess a lot of us are compelled to contribute to the things we love. Does that make any sense?"

GS: "Hey, who's interviewing who here? Let's move on to my next question. Sentient alien robots. Do you ever think we'll find such a thing in our Universe?"

AM: "The Universe is a big place, Garrett, so I don't want to ever say never. I really don't like to make predictions. Most of them are probably wrong. Heck, I can't even predict what I'm having for dinner this time next week. But I would say that whether or not anything like them exists, it will be unlikely for us to meet them in my lifetime."

GS: "Well, we'll probably create them first."

AM: "How do you mean?"

GS: "Oh, you know… ChatGPT and all the Generative AI that's going to take over and destroy our society first."

AM: <chuckles> "While my science fiction novels are far from intended to be predictive of what's going to happen with technology in society, hopefully you can see some glimmer of extrapolations I made. I mean, there's the obvious space station in or around the asteroid belt, the fact that we'll likely attempt to mine the asteroids at some point, and the fact that humans will touch down on Titan someday. But then there's some of the less subtle things with computers…"

GS: "How so?"

AM: "I do firmly believe that natural language interface will become *the* defacto computer interface in the near future. Like next decade of future or so."

GS: "Can you explain more?"

AM: "Absolutely. This is what all the current generative AI stuff is allowing us to do. Get work done on our computers through a natural language description of what we want done. Need an image? Say the words to describe it. Need a video? Also, describe it in words. Need a code snippet for something? Words again. It's almost like when we moved from punch cards to keyboards. And added in a mouse. And many years later, touchscreens."

GS: "So, you're an optimist about humanity's relationship with computers and AI?"

AM: "Yes. And you see some of those positive aspects in the book you're reading. Like when Ruby is programming a VR sim. Sure, I have her doing the familiar old-school typing… but I also have her ask Pippa to perform tasks like create avatars. Everything she asks Pippa to do is via natural language. That is how we'll eventually interact with our phones and devices."

GS: "What do you say to people who are fearful of this technology?"

AM: "I don't. It's really easy to be fearful of things we don't understand. People need time to adjust. They needed time to adjust to email and the internet. I'm going to sit back, relax, and worry about writing my next book."

GS: "Excellent. That was on my list of questions to ask. Is your next book going to be an extension of the Robot Galaxy Series?"

AM: "Remember a minute ago when I said I wasn't good at predicting the future?"

GS: "Yes."

AM: "Well, I can tell you that I have am working on a book that is completely unrelated to the Robot Galaxy Series, although it also features sentient AI. I also have a ton of notes and some outlines for several side novels *in* the Robot Galaxy universe. I think the first one I mentioned will come out first, but I'm not ready to say that for sure yet. I also have this idea for a whole other series that I'm really excited about."

GS: "Sounds like you have no shortage of ideas."

AM: "Tru dat."

GS: "Tru dat?"

AM: "Uh, yeah. Kind of a slang expression from my time that I like to say from time to time because of the funny looks I get."

GS: "Tru dat."

AM: "That's uh, not how you use that—"

GS: "Well, that's all the time we have for today! Thank you, Adeena Mig.. Mi…—Thank you, Adeena!"

* * *

A Word or Two From the Author

Thank you for reading not just *Eleven Little Robots*, but the whole Robot Galaxy Series! At least, I assume you wouldn't have started with book 4. That doesn't usually make much sense, although I have to admit that I accidentally read a sequel once or twice and it turned out okay.

I hope that since you made it this far, you enjoyed it all and are looking forward to whatever is next. What's next is a book that is unrelated to The Robot Galaxy, but then I plan to come back to this universe with some "side" novels and then a second series that takes Ruby and her robots on a brand new adventure.

To ensure you stay updated on book releases:

Join my mailing list at: **https://adeenamignogna.com**

With deepest appreciation,
Adeena

About Adeena

Adeena Mignogna is a physicist and astronomer (by degree) working in aerospace as a Mission Architect, which just means she's been doing it so long they had to give her a fun title. More importantly, she's a long-time science fiction geek with a strong desire to inspire others through speaking and writing about robots, aliens, artificial intelligence, computers, longevity, exoplanets, virtual reality, and more. She writes science fiction novels, to include The Robot Galaxy Series (available on Amazon) and loves spending time with her fellow co-hosts of The BIG Sci-Fi Podcast (available wherever you listen to podcasts)!

Adeena lives in Maryland, USA with her hubby, two kids, a pile of computers, and now two cats, named Ruby and Pearl.

https://adeenamignogna.com

Eleven Little Robots